The House on the Hill

The House on the Hill

JOY BAKER

This edition published 2025
by Living Book Press
Copyright © The Estate of Joy Baker 2025

ISBN: 978-1-76183-079-2 (hardcover)
         978-1-76183-039-6 (softcover)

A catalogue record for this book is available from the National Library of Australia

Contents

The author with Christopher and Carol

The swallows are back at the House on the Hill
And the wind blows free
The sunlight is gold at the House on the Hill
And it shines for me
The flowers are in bud at the House on the Hill
And the birds all sing
The pear tree's in bloom at the House on the Hill
And our hearts take wing...

JOY BAKER

A NOTE FROM THE AUTHOR'S CHILDREN

The House on the Hill and its sequel *Turn on the Sun* tell the story of our lives when we did not go to school.

Our childhood had two very different sides. One is told in our mother's book *Children in Chancery*, where we were relentlessly pursued by the local education authorities. Court cases filled our growing years—long hours waiting in courtrooms, sometimes giving evidence ourselves, even being taken from our beds in the middle of the night while our mother was away. At just five to eight years old, we were followed by photographers, splashed across newspapers, and constantly under pressure from officials.

This book shows the other side—what our mother intended for us. We lived with her, a determined and unconventional woman, in an old farmhouse set in the middle of nowhere. When we first arrived, it had no running water, no electricity, and no toilet. But it was surrounded by rolling countryside and filled with life—cows and horses, turkeys and sheep (sometimes wandering into the house), along with our pets: dogs, cats, rabbits, and gerbils.

Our memories are of long summer days learning as needed, winter snowdrifts taller than ourselves, and evenings alive with beauty. Country life brought both its joys and challenges, alongside fairs, ballets, theatre visits, and agricultural shows—one of us even showed cows.

This was the life our mother envisioned for us, and it is the life we share in these pages.

THE CHILDREN

1

We are Seven

When my husband and I were on our honeymoon, we stayed at a cottage with a dear old lady of seventy, who had brought up a family of six children single-handed. Her husband had left her for another woman when she was expecting her sixth baby, and she had never heard from him since; her only comment on this treatment, looking back over the years, was, "I never blamed him. It was all the woman's fault."

When, thirteen years later, I was left in the same position, only with a seventh baby on the way, I could perhaps more reasonably make the same comment. For the woman in my case wore a black shroud, and her name was Death.

I had chosen for my engagement ring an opal, an iridescent sea-green stone set in a cluster of pearls, because I loved it on sight; but people to whom I showed it were horrified.

"Opals are unlucky," they told me. "And pearls are for tears."

Perhaps they are.

I married my husband—a journalist, twenty years older than myself—for the same reason; and I wore my opal and pearls for the thirteen years of my married life.

When my last baby was three months old, we were living in a rambling Georgian house in a quiet village. My husband had only just returned from an absence of several weeks in Ireland, and I had no warning of what was to come when he went to Eastbourne for the day to interview an eccentric elderly lady who kept dogs.

He returned that evening in a state of collapse, breathing painfully.

1

"One of my usual attacks of bronchitis," he said. He had suffered from these periodically since a serious illness which had resulted in his being invalided out of the Army during the War.

I got him to bed and called the doctor, who looked grave and diagnosed bronchitis—and pneumonia. He left me with instructions to apply hot poultices to his back and chest, and to give M and B tablets every four hours, night and day.

I spent that night sleeping in a chair by my husband's bedside, and waking with a start every hour or so. The doctor came again in the morning and said very little, but as he left he looked at me in a gently pitying way which I felt was tactless at the time, although I was to get used to it in the weeks ahead.

"Keep on with the same treatment," he told me. "There is nothing else we can do."

Late that evening my husband became unconscious. I telephoned the doctor, but he was out. The older children had gone to bed, and the two baby boys were asleep in their cots. Only the most unreassuring sound of my husband's laboured breathing reassured me that he was still alive. The night went on, and became a nightmare.

A cry from one of the babies took me down the passage to their room. When I came back I paused at the bedroom door. The painful breathing was quiet. A dreadful stillness filled the room, like a tangible thing, a presence not only in the room but beating against the dark windows outside. I went to the bedside and bent over my husband. I am not sure, but I think I screamed.

So we were seven; and I was somewhat shaken to find, working it out in the middle of the night some weeks later when I knew there was another baby on the way, that our average age amounted to eleven years.

Geoffrey, my second-in-command, aged twelve, tall and fair—or at least fair where his person was not smudged with tractor-grease, oil or mud, as was usually the case; his interest in farming being only equalled by his interest in words, and his ambition being to become a farmer or a barrister, or preferably both...

Steven, eleven, smaller and lighter-built, with straight brown hair and long dark lashes; as domesticated as Geoffrey was outdoor, with a love of colour and beauty, yet able to cook and serve a meal or scrub a floor with fascinating neatness and efficiency—but he wanted to be an artist, so perhaps, I thought, it's a good thing he can cook and scrub floors…

Victoria, aged nine, with long flame-gold hair and only two ruling passions in her life, babies and horses; she could already look after the babies as well as I could, but I didn't see how I could ever provide her with a horse…

Helen, just eight, resembling Victoria only in the brilliant colour of her hair—but Helen's was a tangled mop of red-gold curls, all wind-tossed and wild, like Helen herself. We had a story in our family that when Helen was a baby the fairies took her away in the night and cast a spell on her, and we found her again the next morning sitting on a red toadstool, half child, half elf, which she has been ever since. She was such a complete contrast to Victoria that we called them Queen Victoria and Nell Gwynn…

Then Christopher, one year old, with silver-fair curls and the expressive sky-blue eyes of a very mischievous angel; and four-month-old Nicholas, with dark curls and midnight blue eyes, the most cuddly pink dumpling that was ever tickled, with two dimples nearly always in evidence and a very engaging small droop to his mouth when they weren't…

And then, of course, me—otherwise our average age would have been only eight.

It was no good worrying about it. We had been used to being on our own for long periods, since my husband's work had involved frequent absences from home; and now there we were, the seven of us; and I was faced with the expired tenancy of our present house which I could no longer afford, and the necessity of finding a new home without delay.

To find a home for a family of our size—plus our ten cats—at a low rent, seemed hopeless; for weeks I answered advertisements and viewed houses, without success, and with increasing urgency; and then someone told me that there was a house in a remote village, belonging to a local farmer, which was standing empty. I telephoned the farmer and asked him if he had a house to let.

"Not that I know of," he replied. I was about to ring off when he added, … "Only that place up the drift that no one will live in…"

"That would be the one," I said. "Is it available?"

"Yes, but you won't want that," he said. "I wanted it for a stock-man, but no one will live up there…"

"But would you let it?" I persisted.

"You'd better go and look at it," he said. "You'd have to put it in order yourself. But if you still want it, ring me again."

So I found the House on the Hill; and we moved in at the spring of the year.

The House on the Hill was not originally called that at all; it was known locally as "That place of Potter's up the drift." I found my way to it with difficulty, after passing it twice without seeing it was there. It was considered so isolated that no one would live in it, and it had stood empty for years past; a small, compact old farmhouse, with the farm buildings, long since fallen into disuse, still grouped comfortably behind it, beside a pond and a group of willow trees. Cattle grazed round it; in fact, when I first saw it, they could and did put their heads through the many broken windows.

Local opinion had been horrified. "You'll never stand living up there," I was told. "It's much too isolated—and they say there's a ghost. The last tenant hanged himself in the barn!"

"Well, I don't suppose he'll hurt us," I said.

"Right up that drift... Falling to pieces..." "Supposed to be haunted"—with these encouraging remarks in my ears I surveyed our future home. There was a fair-sized kitchen, with adjoining dairy; a large living-room with an enormous pantry opening out of it; and upstairs four bedrooms, opening off a minute landing at the top of stairs leading up from the living-room. Two ceilings were down, most of the windows were out; but the walls, about two feet thick, looked as if they had stood for centuries and would stand untouched for centuries more. A wildness of grass all round, coming even into the living-room through the front door; two steep fields between it and the nearest road, and no roadway across to it but "the drift," with rough stones and long grass underfoot, and then a muddy track across the field where the cattle grazed. I looked at it all—and fell in love.

Some things had to be done before we moved in. We had a sink put in the kitchen, with a pump on it piped from the well; we had the dairy converted into a bathroom, with a real bath, although it had to be filled with buckets; we had the ceilings put up and the windows put in, and a concrete path put down outside the back door. The landlord put a fence round where the garden had once been, so the cattle no longer looked through the windows—much to the children's disappointment!—and we took out the old copper in the kitchen and built a small larder cupboard in the corner where it had stood; and then we turned the old pantry into a nursery, where the babies could safely play.

Moving in presented problems. How do you get a houseful of furniture up a steep, muddy track? By tractor and trailer, the last occupants did, we were told. We compromised with a van, plus a horse and cart borrowed from a nearby farm standing by at the bottom of the drift to take things up the field, in case the van got stuck.

The weather, kindly, was dry; the sun shone; there were golden pendant catkins on the willow trees. Everything fitted in; and the pantry made a delightful nursery, its deep shelves filled with the children's toys and the floor space half-filled by Christopher's play-pen, under the low window where, by standing on his bath turned upside-down, he could look out at cattle grazing, moorhens swimming on the pond, and swallows winging overhead.

After the inevitable chaos of moving in, the silence of our isolation was a beautiful peace. I was awakened that first morning by birds chirruping outside my window, so close they seemed to be just over my head. A pair of turtle doves came and sat each morning on the chimney-pot, and cooed down my bedroom chimney; and Steven found he actually had a starling's nest in the tiles immediately above his head, where the ceiling sloped down to within a few feet from the floor, and he could lie and listen to the excited chirping of the baby birds every few minutes when the parents arrived with something to eat, only a few inches from his face.

We were in the middle of our first breakfast when I heard a thump at the back door and went to see who it was, leaving Steven to finish cooking the bacon. I opened the door and there on the threshold stood three large black pigs. Three fat old sows, apparently quite glad to find the house occupied, and with every intention of coming in. I shut the door hastily, and called the family; despatched Geoffrey round our more immediate neighbours to discover the pigs' owner, and Helen to shoo them a little farther away from the door; and returned with Steven and Victoria to our own personal bacon. It was on the table when Geoffrey came back, accompanied by a boy from the nearest farm, and asked if he could help him drive the pigs home. He returned some time later, hungry and muddy.

So, a few minutes after, did the pigs.

I was occupied in driving them away from the back door again when there was a shout from Helen at the front window.

"Look! A man! Two men!"

So there were. Two men working in the ditch of the next field. We all stood and gazed.

"Real people. Up here!" we said.

"They're hedgerers and ditcherers," announced Helen, who frequently makes up words far more expressive than those in more regular use. "Can I go and help them?"

"When we've got rid of the pigs," I said.

"I know where they come from now," said Geoffrey, hastily finishing his breakfast. "I'll take them back."

Quiet again. Steven peeled potatoes for lunch, Victoria and I did the babies' washing, Helen hedgered and ditchered muddily but happily outside, and Christopher watched with great interest from his window.

Lunch was on the table when Geoffrey returned, and I got Helen in and persuaded her to wash off some of the more noticeable mud.

"I've been helping to fence in the pigs," Geoffrey explained. "What do we do this afternoon?"

"Go exploring," I said. "I want to find the station, and all I know is it's somewhere out at the back of us."

"Which do you call the back?" Geoffrey inquired.

A reasonable question, because our back door faced over the main approach to the house, which I called the front, while the front door looked out over fields and an even muddier, more deeply-rutted and overgrown "drift" known as "the loke," and leading to places then unknown.

Twelve-year-old Geoffrey

Eleven-year-old Steven

Nine-year-old Victoria

Eight-year-old Helen

Eighteen-month-old Christopher

The author with six-month-old Nicholas

The House on the Hill

"I mean the back way out of the front door," I said.

"I see," said Geoffrey, "past those cottages."

We were all intrigued by the cottages. We could see two chimneys sticking up through the trees only a little way up "the loke," but no sign of any inhabitants.

So after lunch, the four elder children set off, and I took Christopher for a walk in his push-chair down the road, and then settled down in the biggest arm-chair with four of our ten cats, and darned stockings until they returned.

"We found the station," they all informed me at once. "You go down the loke until you come to a road, and first we went left until we didn't come to anything but two houses, quite a long way down, and then we turned back and went right, and passed two farms, and down a hill past another farm, and the station is right at the bottom of the hill."

"And what about the cottages?" I said.

"Oh, they *aren't* cottages any more," said Steven. "The doors are all off and the staircases have fallen in and most of the inside walls and floors are down. No one could have lived there for years."

"And I thought they were our nearest neighbours," I said.

"But we found some palm," said Victoria, and held out a bunch of gold and silver, kitten soft.

"I think that's nicer than people," I said.

There was a scuffle and thump at the back door.

"Go and see what *that* is," I said to Geoffrey.

He came back laughing. "It's our nearest neighbours," he said. "I told them that fence wouldn't hold long. Shall I take them back again?"

"Yes, you'd better," I said, and Victoria and I started preparing tea, while Geoffrey and Steven and Helen set off down the field, driving three large black pigs.

2

Danger—Cattle Crossing

That was our first day at the House on the Hill. To begin with, the absence of any human neighbours did seem queer, if not actually particularly unpleasing. We awarded points to members of the family who did meet a human being on our hill-top—one point for seeing one, and two for actually exchanging conversation; and we never saw any sign of the rumoured ghostly tenant in the barn—only the old farm implements, and our cats asleep in the straw.

Disadvantages there certainly were, but mostly ones that only needed getting used to. Schools were a long way away; but this appeared to me—and to the children—to be an advantage rather than the reverse, since I felt that any irregularities in their formal learning would be more than compensated for by the increased experience of tackling life hand-to-hand which they would gain from our new circumstances, and that this did in any case constitute a valuable part of their education. I had found throughout my own life that most of the things I was taught in school had never been of the slightest use to me, and I had always felt that a practical training in everyday things was of quite as much value to most children as the patchwork of subjects pushed into their minds in school. The education authorities, however, did not agree with my views, and there were continual verbal arguments and more or less acrimonious correspondence, and even an occasional appearance in the local Court; none of which did anything to alter either my views or those of the authorities.

Tradesmen's deliveries were no longer the straightforward matter they used to be. Our grocer drove his van up the field, unless it was very wet—then he walked. The baker didn't like the idea of driving up—he had a new van. So we had a safe put up on the roadside at the bottom of the drift, and he left the bread there for us to collect. The milkman didn't like the idea of driving up either, visualizing his van overturned and hundreds of smashed milk bottles, and this presented us with the problem of getting eight pints of milk up the field daily; which we solved by getting the milkman to leave the milk in a crate, and using a barrow to bring it up the field.

It was obviously going to be impossible to get a coal lorry up the field—except in summer, when we shouldn't need to. We had nowhere to store a bulk delivery of coal, and couldn't fetch up hundredweight sacks from the road by tractor, as the last occupants had done. So we gave up the idea of using coal, and arranged to heat the house by oil. We found that a glowing paraffin fire in the sitting-room was just as warm as a real fire, and had the additional advantage that I only had to light it when I came down in the mornings, and, provided we remembered to keep it filled once a day, it never went out. There still remained the problem of getting the paraffin up the field; but our local supplier, like the grocer, drove up when it was fine, and carried up the five-gallon can when it was wet. And we could always fetch a gallon at a time from the shop.

Laundry presented an even odder problem, since the nearest stopping point of our local laundry was about half a mile down the road. This we got over by arranging to leave our laundry each week for collection in a cart-shed conveniently situated on the corner passed by the laundry van, and taking it to and fro on the barrow. No one seemed to find anything unusual in this, and we soon came to refer to the cart-shed as "the laundry" in ordinary conversation. When the farm it belonged to changed hands, it was a long time before I learned the name of the new owner, although I waved to his wife every time I went down with the barrow; and we simply referred to her as "Mrs Laundry."

People soon ceased to be everyday occurrences; but there were quite a lot of us, after all, and it never seemed to matter very much. Our neighbours were pigs, sheep, horses, and cows. Every evening during our first summer, the cows would start a procession from our field to the big field beyond the pond, passing our front windows on the way. Outside the front windows were two large apple trees, and there the cows all stopped to have their evening back-scratch. Early in the mornings they went back past our windows again, and as I lay in bed I could hear their gentle breathing as they passed. It is one of the nicest ways I know of being awakened in the morning. Nicholas would lie in his cot and listen, chuckling, while Christopher watched through the bars of his cot. I think the animals were glad to have someone living in the house again.

They also continued to provide interest in ways that human neighbours seldom do. One morning I was hanging out the washing, while Steven and the girls took Christopher in his push-chair and picked hogweed for our landlord's rabbits, when I heard a persistent mooing coming from the fields behind the house. After a time it became impossible to ignore it, so I sent Geoffrey to investigate. He came back to say that one of "our" cows had broken through into a neighbouring field—and was calling frantically to the rest of them.

"If she isn't got back quickly, they'll all break through to join her," he pointed out. "But I can't get her back by myself."

It was a nice warm day and I'd just finished the washing.

"All right," I said. "I'll come and help."

I picked up a stick out of the hedge, and we set off down the big field. I hadn't been there before, and found it a lovely stretch of tussocky grass, with bushes and hummocks and little hills, and paths made by cattle and sheep—a perfect children's playground. To get through to the adjoining field, where the cow was, we had to go right to the bottom. Here there was a gap in the hedge, where crushed brambles and hoof-marks in the mud showed clearly where the cow had got through.

"We'll have to drive her back here," Geoffrey said. "There's no other way through the hedge."

The cow was walking distractedly up and down the hedge at the top end of the field.

Geoffrey and I pushed through the gap and started to walk up the field. Suddenly the cow caught sight of us, and putting her head down tore down the field towards us at considerable speed.

"It's a good thing you brought that stick," Geoffrey remarked calmly. "This cow is apt to be difficult and bad-tempered at times."

I looked apprehensively at the cow, which was now bearing down on us rapidly and with every appearance of animosity. I stood still.

"Look, Geoffrey," I said, "do you mean to tell me you've brought me out here in my present condition to play toreador to a charging and angry cow?"

"Oh, I don't think she's dangerous," said Geoffrey cheerfully. "She's just bad-tempered when she gets upset."

"I don't see the distinction," I said crossly; and made a dive for the hedge. It was a thorny, prickly one, and I backed into it with difficulty, while Geoffrey, much amused, stood guard over me with the stick.

The cow came upon us with a thunder of hooves—and rushed straight past. In point of fact, she didn't even look at us, other than a glance in passing, but made straight for the gap in the hedge which we had been intending to drive her through. By the time Geoffrey had extricated me from the hedge—and removed sundry thorns from my clothes and hair—she had pushed her way back through the gap and rejoined the herd.

We walked back after her, with brambles still sticking into me at various points, and after scrambling through it again, did what we could to block up the gap in the hedge.

"Next time I go cow-chasing with you," I told Geoffrey, "kindly tell me when you expect the cow to be bad-tempered *first*."

"Well," said Geoffrey pointedly, "she's in calf—and they *do* get difficult then, don't they?"

I couldn't think of any adequate reply to this, except "Moo!"—and a newly sympathetic glance at the now quietly grazing cow, as we walked peacefully back up the hill to the house.

3

Rubella

It was late spring, and Geoffrey's birthday. We went to town for the day, and spent half an hour looking round the museum, following after a party of forty or so schoolchildren being taken round on a conducted tour.

Two weeks later, Geoffrey woke up feeling ill. I kept him in bed, but no definite symptoms became apparent until midday, when I found his chest and back covered in spots. I telephoned the doctor, whom we had not previously seen. He arrived in the middle of the afternoon, and demanded to know, very crossly, why I hadn't rung up before ten o'clock.

I replied that the spots hadn't developed until twelve noon, to which he replied that *all* calls for a doctor to visit should be made before ten o'clock in the morning.

Somewhat irritated, I responded that this would mean living through the looking-glass—first call the doctor, then develop the symptoms, and, of course, the actual illness comes last of all...

With this promising beginning we went upstairs to Geoffrey's room.

After an inspection the doctor announced, "German measles—there's a lot of it about," and added cheerfully, "You'll probably all get it—nothing to worry about—it's only serious during pregnancy."

I saw Geoffrey's face go white, and my mouth felt dry. I said stiffly, "I am pregnant." The doctor looked at me sharply. "How long?" "About two months."

"Well, you're almost certain to get it," he said. "If you do, we

shall have to see about terminating the pregnancy—you don't want
to run the risk of having a deformed child."

But I do, I thought desperately. I want the child I'm carrying,
and how can you be sure it will be deformed? It would be so dreadful never to know what you have destroyed—it might have *wanted*
to live, even if there was something wrong with it—it might be a
perfectly normal child—anyway surely it would be better to wait
and *see*…

But the fear in Geoffrey's eyes hurt, and I only said, "Well, I
haven't got it yet—and anyway," with a sudden gleam of hope—
both Geoffrey and Steven *had* German measles when they were
babies—can you have it twice?

"No—it must have been measles they had then," he responded
infuriatingly. "There isn't a single case of measles in this area just
now"—and I had no chance to suggest that there has to be a first
case of everything anywhere, because he was by then half out of
the back door. I watched him down the field with alternating anger
and panic in my heart.

Geoffrey was waiting for me when I got back upstairs, with an
agonized face. "Does it mean you'll get it and it will hurt the baby?
Why does it? What will they have to do to it?"

"It doesn't mean anything really, darling," I soothed him as best
I could. "I shan't get it, for a start—I never do get things—and
I won't let them touch the baby if I do. It may be quite all right,
they can't know, and anyway, I don't believe you have German
measles—it looks much more like ordinary measles to me."

"That would be all right, wouldn't it?" he asked hopefully.

"Well—you would be much more ill, probably," I said, "but it
would be all right for the baby."

He shut his eyes and turned his face into the pillow. "I hope
it's measles," he said.

I went downstairs quickly, because I didn't want him to see I
was crying…

The next day another doctor turned up—the doctor's assistant,
a much younger man. He looked at Geoffrey, looked puzzled, and
said, "This looks to me like ordinary measles—I've never seen a
case of German measles like it."

"That's what *I* said," I told him triumphantly. "But yesterday the doctor insisted that it was."

"Well, there's a lot of German measles about, certainly," he said. "That's why he would think of that at first—but this doesn't look like it to me—has the boy been out anywhere recently?"

I told him about the museum and the school party.

"Well, that's probably where he got it," he said.

"You mean you think it is ordinary measles then?" I asked.

"Well, I think so," he replied. "But I can't be sure yet—I'll come again tomorrow. If the spots have gone by then, it's German measles—but if they're still as bad as this, it's not."

The next twenty-four hours seemed very long. When I woke the next morning I went in to Geoffrey. He was already awake—trying to look at his chest. Terrified, I looked—the spots were still there, and, if anything, they were worse.

"Well—you've still got them," I said unsteadily. He lay there and smiled. "*Really?*" he said. "I thought I had, but I couldn't see properly—how soon will the doctor come, so we're sure?"

The doctor came mid-morning. He took one look.

"Oh, well, it's measles all right," he said.

Geoffrey listened to the verdict that he knew meant more suffering for him with shining eyes.

When the doctor had gone he said, "Even if you get it, it can't hurt the baby now, can it?"

"No, darling, it *can't*," I said. And for the second time I had to go downstairs quickly to hide tears.

It seemed only fair that Geoffrey was not very ill with measles. After the first few days he improved steadily and had no complications, and he was allowed up on the seventh day.

Three days after he got up, I felt ill. I stayed in bed, only getting up to deal with essentials, while Victoria and Steven ran the household; but the next day I felt better, and I hadn't any symptoms of anything that I could see, so I got up. That day Steven had a sore throat.

The next day Steven was in bed.

The day after that, Steven, Victoria, Helen, and I were all in bed, and Geoffrey telephoned for the doctor. He came and took one look at us. We *all* had measles.

Geoffrey was left to look after the lot of us—and the babies.

The first days were not so bad, because none of us, except the babies, wanted anything to eat. Geoffrey went shopping, washed nappies, got his own meals, brought us glasses of water, administered our medicine after fetching it from the doctor's surgery, and fed the babies after bringing them to me to dress or change. He got up at six and went to bed at ten, and throughout the long day I never once called to him, which it seemed to me I had to do continually about something or other, without getting a cheerful response. The house seemed very quiet and I felt too ill to wonder very much what was happening to everyone else. Geoffrey brought me in periodical reports, mostly that the others were asleep. It was all like a very bad dream.

After a day or two we all got hungry. Geoffrey was no good at cooking except in a rough-and-ready masculine way, and he started worrying. So I put on a dressing-gown and he helped me downstairs and held me up while I prepared a chicken casserole. I got it into the oven and staggered back to bed. Two hours later Geoffrey served it, and I was encouraged by calls of appreciation from Steven. Geoffrey said the girls enjoyed it too, but Victoria ate very little.

That evening Geoffrey had to go to the doctor's surgery to fetch some medicine. He left us all comfortable and I was half asleep. Sounds on the landing woke me and I heard footsteps going down the stairs. I called out and a small voice answered me. It was Victoria going to the bathroom. Of course she shouldn't have done so and I blamed myself for being asleep when I should have stopped her. I called again anxiously, and heard footsteps returning. Then there was a slithering noise and a bump—and nothing more.

I got out of bed and ran downstairs. Victoria lay unconscious on the sitting-room floor.

I was shaking all over, and wasn't sure if I had enough strength to get back up the stairs myself, after using the energy of panic that had brought me down. But there was no one I could call and I couldn't just leave her lying there. Somehow I managed to pick her up, pathetically white and still but appallingly heavy, and step by step staggered up the stairs with her in my arms.

I shall never know how I got her back into bed. But I did, and I tucked her in and sat down heavily on the bed, feeling that I could never stand up again. Her eyelids flickered open and she said, "What happened?"

"You fainted," I said. "But you're quite all right, my sweet. You mustn't try to go downstairs till you're better. Lie down now and go to sleep."

She lay back and I looked at the tangle of golden hair over the pillow. She put up a hand to it. "My hair is dreadfully tangly," she said faintly. "I couldn't do it, and it feels all knots."

"Never mind," I said. "I'll brush it for you tomorrow."

We were all in bed for a week, and Steven for ten days, because he seemed likely to develop bronchitis. When I was able to brush Victoria's hair properly it was so knotted that I couldn't get brush or comb through it, and had to cut the worst tangles away. But she had so much hair that it didn't seem to make any difference.

A few days after we were up again, Christopher and Nicholas both came out in spots. But they had it very mildly, and apart from wanting only half their normal meals for several days, showed no other ill effects.

And, as Geoffrey said, if we hadn't been so bad it would have been much worse. At least we knew that I hadn't had German measles. And we all felt that, after surviving all that, we could survive anything.

4

Tin Cans and Wild Horses

When we had all recovered from the measles, we started to think about the garden. At least, we turned our attention to where the garden had been, and ought presumably to be. The only beauty about it at that time was the apple trees. There were ten, old, twisted ones, clustered round the house, and when they were all covered in blossom we were enveloped in a pink and white mist. It was like living in a chaffinches' nest.

But when the blossom fell, in one of the violent hail and wind storms of late spring, it was a depressing prospect. Grass, trampled by the cattle and full of thistles and nettles; piles of rubble left by the builders; piles of assorted junk left by, it seemed, all the other occupants of long ago.

Obviously, the first thing to do was to get rid of the junk. No dustcart could get up our field, but we carried the dustbins down to the roadside every two weeks for collection. We could do the same with the accumulation of junk.

So we started, pulling out the most extraordinary collection of half-buried articles: bits of a bedstead, bits of a bicycle, teapots, kettles, saucepans, jugs, buckets, all rusty or broken; bottles, jam-jars, and old tin cans—there were literally hundreds of tin cans. At first we moved the things that lay in piles; then we dug, and found more and more—it seemed it would never end. We were, in fact, shifting a rubbish dump that had accumulated from many families over years and years. Barrow-load after barrow-load Geoffrey and Steven carted down to the roadside—where the grass verge soon began to look more like the aftermath of a bomb. But the dustmen did take it away; and we did get our garden clear at last.

Standing in the middle of the biggest hollow we had caused, where at last our spade turned over earth instead of clanging into bottles and tins, I surveyed the prospects. A fat robin also surveyed the results of our work with satisfaction—the earth was full of big fat worms.

"Bluebells," I said to Steven. "We'll have bluebells here—and flowering shrubs—and nasturtiums. We'll cover it with nasturtiums."

The next thing was the builders' rubble—and paths. These, I pointed out to Steven, went together; we got rid of the rubble by putting it down to make paths.

After that came flower beds. Geoffrey was no gardener, and after the initial spade-work was over he preferred to go and help on the farm. Steven and I set to work to dig out flower beds in the grass. My planning of these was quite simple—I dug flower beds wherever the grass was too thin or too bumpy to be worth keeping, in whatever shape this occurred; and the results were unexpectedly attractive, providing beds in graceful curves round winding paths as well as straight borders and formal beds; while the remaining grass too, looked distinctly more hopeful, viewed as a potential lawn.

Steven, Victoria, and I collected all the big stones and bricks we could find, and edged the flower beds with them. We then started to acquire flowers. But as, apart from the apple trees, there was nothing in the garden but grass, nettles and thistles, it took some time to make any effect.

I gave Steven a bit of fairly fine earth—most of the garden being heavy clay—for a seed bed, and he sowed lettuces, carrots, spring onions, and radishes. Only the lettuces came up; but these did so well that he eventually transplanted one hundred and fifty into one of the new flower beds.

I bought nasturtium seeds—packets and packets—and put them in all over the ex-rubbish dump. They came up—they produced thousands of leaves, which were an improvement on the tin cans—and then they flowered. They flooded the rubbish dump with scarlet and amber and gold—and spread out over the paths and the grass—they climbed up the apple trees and shook out gay orange dusters from every branch. Victoria and I could look at them from the kitchen window as we did the washing; and every so often she and Steven and I would stop whatever we were doing and say, "Oh, look at our nasturtiums!"

We got a pair of shears, and started clipping down the grass, yard by yard. Our great day came when we got a lawn mower—and actually managed to push it over the best parts of the grass. It was heavy going, but after several evenings' work with the shears, followed by the mower, we did get something really looking like a lawn.

By this time Steven and I were acutely garden-conscious, and began waking up in the night if there was a heavy rain, or if we heard cats fighting or cows mooing, in fear that something might damage our precious seed beds or grass. Keeping the cattle out, which hadn't really bothered us before, now became a matter of vital urgency. Steven and I got up in the middle of one night to chase out a cow who had pushed open our gate and was standing just inside, contemplating our flowers.

A herd of young bullocks put on the field did nothing to add to our peace of mind, and when they showed every sign of preferring the look of the grass in our garden to that in the field, we grew quite frantic, and, like David Copperfield's aunt and the donkeys, I was perpetually calling out, "Steven! Bullocks!" whenever I saw one approaching our fence.

Soon after the bullocks' arrival, two large cart-horses were put on our field, one brown and one grey. The grey was nervous and excitable, but the brown was steady and friendly, with a most endearing bristly moustache. We called him George.

Victoria spent most of her free time with him. She sat on his back for hours while he stood under the willow trees, or waded into the pond and stood getting cool in the still water, and rode him round the field whenever he was willing to go for a walk. He was so big that she could not get on him unaided, but Helen or one of the boys was usually available to give her a leg up, or she persuaded him to come up to a fence or gate from which she could mount.

One afternoon I was alone in the house with the babies; the boys and Helen were out hogweeding, and Victoria went as usual to play with George. Suddenly her face appeared at the open window.

"Do you think you could help me on? He won't come up to the fence, and when I took the steps over to him he was frightened and backed away."

The idea of going up to a large horse with a pair of household steps was irresistible. I said I would see what I could do, and went with her to where the horse grazed peacefully in the middle of the field. But I was in no condition to lift Victoria's weight up on to his back—I hadn't the necessary spring.

"You might do what Helen does," Victoria said doubtfully. "She bends down so I can stand on her back, and then I jump on."

"Well," I said, "I'll try."

I bent over, not without difficulty, beside the horse.

"I'll take my boots off—they're muddy," said Victoria.

Then she climbed on to my back. I couldn't see what was happening, but there was a cry from Victoria, "Can you move nearer? He's walking away!"

I looked up, and saw George grazing leisurely away from us. Bent double, I followed, with Victoria on my back. The horse quickened his step—so did I. Victoria gave a sudden spring off my shoulders, and landed sideways on the horse. I straightened myself up and gave her a push into position. She scrambled upright and we looked at each other breathlessly.

"Thank you," said Victoria. "Oh—where are my boots?"

I collected them from our starting point some way up the field, and put them on her feet. Already lost in dreams, her hair a golden cloud about her face, she and George ambled away.

I made my way back to the house. Halfway across the field, I became aware of a man in a grey suit surveying me incredulously from our garden gate. When I reached him I found it was our landlord, come to see how we were getting on. I don't think he had quite believed his own eyes when he saw me on all fours, with Victoria on my back, apparently having a race with the horse…

Usually when Victoria rode the brown horse the grey one ignored them. But at times it became disgruntled, and galloped round until the brown horse joined it, apparently jealous of its companion's growing affection for Victoria.

One afternoon I saw Victoria setting off for their usual peaceful

The House—so isolated that no one else would live in it

The 'loke' … and our nearest neighbours

Christopher taking the empty milk bottles down the field
and putting them in the safe by the road

walk round the field. A little while later I was startled by the loud thunder of hooves galloping past our windows. I ran out, and was more than startled to see both horses galloping wildly round the field—and Victoria still on the brown horse's back. How she stayed on, without saddle or bridle, I don't know. She was clinging to his mane, perched on a back as broad as a table, but she stayed there, her hair flying out behind. A beautiful picture—but a terrifying sight. I called Geoffrey and Steven—but how do you stop two playful cart-horses? It seemed hours before they slowed down, and Victoria slid off, and ran to us with shining eyes.

"He *galloped*!" she said.

The next afternoon she went out to give the horse a lump of sugar. A few minutes later Helen ran in. "Come quickly! George is *in our garden*!"

"Oh, no!" I said, and ran out to see.

And there he was.

He stood in the middle of our lawn. In a smaller space he looked enormous. Victoria was patting his nose. She turned to me—"I couldn't help it—I was giving him sugars at the gate, and he just *came* in!"

"Well—can you get him to go *out*?" I said.

"No—he won't!" said Victoria.

She caught hold of his forelock and pulled. Helen got behind him and pushed. George looked benignly at both of them—and moved two steps sideways, towards my precious nasturtiums.

"Stop him!" I cried. "Our flower-beds!"

The horse bent his head and took a mouthful of grass. Steven went to his head and tugged. It was like trying to move an oak tree.

Helen said, "Shall I get a stick?"

Geoffrey said, "No—you can't drive a horse with a stick. He'll just run wild all over the place."

"Perhaps if you offered him some more sugar?" I suggested.

"I've tried," said Victoria. She held out the sugar on her hand and moved towards the gate. The horse looked hopefully at it, and waited patiently for her to feed it to him.

"If only we had a halter," she said.

"There used to be an old rope halter in the barn," said Steven.

"Well, get it!" I said —

"—but I've looked, and it isn't there now," he concluded.

"Couldn't we *make* one with string?" said Victoria.

Geoffrey felt in his pockets and produced a tattered piece of binder twine. "This wouldn't be strong enough, would it?" he said.

"We can try it," said Steven. He took the twine and twisted it and tied a few knots, and with the resultant sort of cat's cradle went up to the horse, and slipped it over his nose and behind his ears. Victoria took hold of it and pulled gently.

"Come on," she said, "this way."

George moved obediently forward, and, with the apparently magic string hanging over his face, he followed her unhesitatingly—over the grass, down the path, through the gate.

"I can ride him with this," said Victoria happily, and she and Helen disappeared, leading the horse, into the big field. I went back to the babies.

Victoria came in an hour or so later to help me get the babies' tea. "We had a lovely ride," she said. "With the halter, I got him to trot."

"Where's Helen?" I asked.

"She wanted to stay out longer," said Victoria. "She's still with George."

We got on with the evening baby-time, and until Christopher and Nicholas were bathed I forgot about Helen. By then it was getting dark, and she still hadn't come in.

"Geoffrey, go and call Helen," I said. "She should be in by now."

He was back in a few minutes, looking puzzled. "I found her in the barn, crying," he said, "but she won't say why."

I ran out, to find Helen on the doorstep. She was covered in mud, and shivering and sobbing violently.

"My darling, what is it?" I said, and put my arms round her. She clung tightly round my neck, but wouldn't speak. I carried her in.

All kinds of terrors began to go round in my mind. She was so terribly distressed—what could have happened to her, in the big field on our lonely hill? I nursed her in my arms, but she wouldn't answer my anxious questions—until at last she whispered, "I don't want the others to know."

Still frightened and knowing I mustn't show it, I carried her into the bathroom. She sat on my knee and went on sobbing.

"Please darling—tell me what happened," I said.

She gasped back tears.

"I was sitting on the horse," she said, "and it got quite dark, and I was watching the lights in the houses all round come on…" —she clutched my neck— "—and I fell asleep, and I must have fallen off his back, and when I woke up I was lying on the wet grass, and I couldn't think where I was!"

Relief struggled with incredulity in my mind.

"Don't you remember falling off the horse, or hitting the ground?"

She shook her head.

"No—I remember watching the lights, and then I woke up on the grass, and I couldn't remember where I was until I saw George looking at me!"

She buried her face in my neck again. "Don't tell the others!" she whispered.

I started to laugh, and dried her tears, and carried her back into the sitting-room. We got her wet clothes off her and put her straight into Nicholas' still-warm bath.

By the time she was dry and in her nightdress, she had recovered, and started to see the funny side of it; and sitting by the fire afterwards eating a boiled egg, was telling the others about it herself.

"What will the girls do with that horse next!" said Geoffrey. "But only *Helen* could *fall* asleep on a horse!"

5

Looking Back

As far back as I can remember, I wanted to have ten children, while I was young enough to be still young and active while they were all growing up. No one to whom I have told this, from doctors onwards, has ever been anything but astounded, sometimes even quite horrified, predicting my "wearing myself out" with child-bearing—although everyone has had to admit that I have survived so far without any noticeable signs of permanent wear and tear.

I started my family when I was twenty-one, in a town near London, during the last months of the war, which still cast its greyly unreal effect over everything. I had never read any literature about having babies or on child care, and, not being a sociable person, I had no circle of friends and acquaintances with whom to exchange experiences and views. I regarded having babies as a purely natural function, like breathing, and cats having kittens; and my main reason for going to a doctor when I first thought I *was* pregnant, was to get confirmation that I was pregnant, and my certificate for extra milk.

The doctor agreed that I probably was, but he refused to give me a certificate without making an internal examination first. I reluctantly agreed to this, after which he said that he still couldn't be sure, but he would give me the certificate anyway.

I went home, feeling odd and uncomfortable inside. When I got in I found I was losing a little blood. I went to bed and kept my feet up, but the bleeding continued, and my husband sent for the doctor, who came and said I was starting a miscarriage. He added, did I really want the baby?—because if not he could bring on the miscarriage and get rid of it.

I imagine the horror and distress in my face gave him sufficient answer. I told him I wanted the baby with all my heart—and broke down in tears. He gave me an injection which he said should help to stop the miscarriage; but it didn't. The bleeding increased, and I lost my baby the following day.

Nothing that had ever happened to me had hurt me more, and I still feel there is another child in my family, the baby I already loved and never saw. The doctor was not only obstetrically clumsy, but cruelly tactless—he let me lie in bed and hear the sound of his dropping what would have been my child down the adjoining lavatory.

I recovered quickly from the miscarriage, but the hurt didn't start to heal until I knew, two months later, that I was pregnant again.

This time I refused to have any examination, and kept away from the doctor. I had never heard of ante-natal care then, and apparently the doctor hadn't either, for he did not ask to see me, after giving me my milk certificate, until a month before the baby was due to be born. Then he wanted to examine me internally, but I was still so frightened by my last experience that I flatly refused; and he compromised with an X-ray. This showed that the baby was lying perfectly, but the doctor said I appeared to be very small inside and he thought a Caesarian operation might be advisable, as he was doubtful if I could have a normal delivery. In the end he decided that I could; and I didn't see him again until the date he had told me the baby should be born.

Then he walked in and said, rather in the manner of someone who has placed an order for goods and is waiting for delivery, what was I doing about this baby?

I wasn't doing anything except carrying on with my normal daily activities, a little (but not very much) slower than usual, and waiting contentedly for the baby to be born; but he expressed concern at its not coming on time, and said that if it was not born during that week it might be too big to be born at all.

Having thoroughly frightened my husband and myself, he left, telling us to get the nurse in immediately (I was having a monthly nurse for the confinement) and to follow her advice to hasten the baby's arrival. It wasn't until some time later that we learned there was another reason for the doctor's concern that the baby should be born before the end of the week—the coming weekend should have been his weekend off.

The nurse, an elderly little Irishwoman, suggested long bumpy bus rides, and gave me enemas and castor oil and hot baths, and generally kept me in a state of acute physical discomfort and mental unrest for the next week. And then, when apparently she couldn't think of anything else to do to me, and ten days after the date of the baby's expected arrival, while I was lying peacefully on the settee in the sitting-room at five o'clock one evening, I had a pain in my back which was unlike any pain I had ever had before in my life, but which somehow I recognized immediately; and I knew that my baby was on the way at last.

After a number of pains, I went and told the nurse that I had started labour.

"Nonsense!" she said, after one look at me. "You wouldn't be so cheerful about it if you had."

I went back to the sitting-room and went on quietly having pains. A little later she came in and saw me in the middle of one— and hastily started to prepare my bedroom for the baby's birth, saying, well, perhaps I was in labour after all.

At eleven o'clock that night the waters broke, and the nurse told me to start pushing. That night was the longest in my whole life. I went on all night long, while the nurse trotted backwards and forwards bringing what seemed to me to be the entire contents of my kitchen in the way of bowls, jugs and so on into the bedroom, and urging me each time she came in to go on pushing; which I was doing anyway, with all my strength at every pain.

During the small hours of the morning I started asking, "How much longer should it be, nurse?" and my husband started asking, "Oughtn't you to send for the doctor?"

"Oh, I can't tell how much longer it will be yet," she kept telling us. "We don't want to disturb the doctor yet, I'll send for him all in good time."

The darkness wore away and early daylight began to lighten the sky. By then I was so weak with exhaustion that it was an enormous effort to stir myself to push with each pain, and I fell into a heavy sleep between each one.

At seven o'clock, the nurse agreed to send for the doctor. When he came, he said the baby's head was right down, but he didn't think I would be able to get it out myself before midday—would I agree to having an anaesthetic?

By then I would probably have agreed to being hit over the head with a brick.

There was a further delay while he fetched the anaesthetist, of whom I remember nothing except that he was wearing a bright pink scarf—I was more than half unconscious with pain and exhaustion already. The pink scarf floated away and took the dark night with it. I remembered nothing more until the doctor's voice drifted momentarily back into my consciousness—"I'm afraid the baby's dead, nurse…" —then I slid away into utter blackness.

When I awoke again the sun was shining into my bedroom and the night had gone forever—but leaving behind it, as I remembered the doctor's words, the more terrible blackness of despair. Convinced that my baby was dead, I dared not ask, afraid that no one would tell me yet anyway; I lay there, too weak to move, even to lift my head—until, away in the next room, I heard—I was *sure* I heard!—a baby cry.

A little later the nurse came in, and I said to her weakly, "Have I *really* had a baby?"

"Yes, of course," she said, "an eight-pound boy."

"And—he's alive?"

"Of course he's alive—didn't you hear him just now be crying in his bath?"

And then she brought Geoffrey to me, and I gazed at the most wonderful sight any woman can ever look upon—my new-born child. He had golden fluff and wide blue eyes, and was pink and uncrumpled like a new rose petal.

The doctor told me later that he had thought he was dead when he was first born because he didn't cry; and that if I had gone on any longer in labour, he *would* have died.

While I lay in bed that day, being dug into painfully by five stitches, and having to be held up to have a drink because I was still too weak to lift my own head, I remember thinking, "Perhaps I'll have only *seven* babies, not ten."

But such is the resilience of youth that within a few days I was fed up with being in bed and wanting to work off my surplus energy, and kept asking the nurse, "When can I get up?"

Both doctor and nurse insisted that I must not put my feet to the ground for two weeks; but I couldn't wait until then, and I compromised by dropping out of bed on my hands and knees when the nurse was out of the way, and getting about the room like that—so I wasn't really "putting my feet to the ground"—and climbing back into bed again before anyone came.

On the fourteenth day the nurse made me wait in bed until the doctor arrived; he came in, looked at me, and said, yes, I could get up, and went downstairs. He had not reached the front door by the time I had got out of bed, dressed, and run down too. He looked at me in some surprise, and said he hadn't meant I could get up straight away like that.

But I was on my feet again, and I stayed there. The nurse predicted dire consequences if I did too much the first day, but, perhaps because I had already been getting a good deal of exercise which she didn't know about, I felt perfectly fit from then on; and my next concern was to get rid of the nurse. She left at the end of the month, and I had my baby to myself at last.

Geoffrey was born on my twenty-second birthday; perhaps that was what he was waiting for. I fed him myself as long as I had milk; then, at five months, I had to wean him, and a month later Steven was on the way.

By then we had moved into a new house in the country, and the woman doctor who attended me there had a very different approach to the one in town. When I told her of my previous experiences, she examined me carefully—externally—and told me she could see no reason why I should not have a normal delivery, without instruments or anaesthetic, this time.

"I shan't even bring my forceps," she said.

I started labour at midday, on the exact date that Steven was due to be born; the nurse came in, and I kept on my feet for several hours, until the pains gradually increased, and I went to bed. At six o'clock, the nurse sent for the doctor; she arrived breathless, having hurried from her evening surgery, and showed me how to work gas and air apparatus. Then the waters broke, and she told me to turn on my back and push. I had one pain, and when I pushed it didn't hurt any more. The doctor said, "Good! The head's down. Push hard next time."

The pain came, and I pushed, and I saw Steven born. I felt his tiny body warm and soft against my legs, and heard his first cry. I called to my husband, who had only just retired to the sitting-room prepared for a long wait, "The baby's here! It's another boy!"

When Victoria was born, sixteen months after Steven, I didn't even have a doctor to attend the birth. I got in a fully qualified midwife, and my doctor gave me my routine ante-natal examinations and sent the midwife a report, and we hired gas and air apparatus on her authority.

On the day Victoria was due, I had one definite pain at seven o'clock in the evening; and then nothing more until ten o'clock that night, by which time we had given up waiting and gone to bed. Then I started labour.

Most of the early stages I spent lying in bed watching my husband and the midwife trying to get the gas and air apparatus to work; until suddenly the pains changed, the waters broke, the midwife shoo'ed my husband out of the room, and Victoria was there. As for the gas and air, we found afterwards that the cylinder we had connected was, by some oversight, empty. But I got the air all right.

By the time I was expecting Helen, fifteen months later, I felt I knew something about having babies, and was looking forward to her birth. By then we had moved again to a new home; I had arranged to have the same midwife who delivered Victoria, but she was taken ill at the last moment, and I had to get in a strange nurse, who was however fully qualified to undertake the delivery. She was quite young, and I got the impression when she first arrived that she was worried about something; I didn't realize until it was too late that what she was worried about was delivering me.

Helen did not show any signs of arriving until two weeks after the date on which she was due, and during the time we were waiting the nurse became increasingly nervous. I eventually started labour in the middle of the night, and when we called the nurse she appeared to be afraid that I might have the baby at any moment, although I assured her that I had several hours to go. She called the local doctor, a kind, comfortable man, who came and said that my estimate was correct, and that he would come back as soon as he was needed for the baby's birth.

It was a beautiful spring night, and I lay in bed contentedly through the early stages of labour, listening to a soft rain falling outside, thinking of my baby coming into that damp, sweet-smelling world.

Then daylight came, touching everything with silvery warmth; and the pains changed, and I knew the baby was nearly there.

I called to the nurse, who had already telephoned for the doctor, "We shan't be able to wait for him to come. I think the baby will be here with the next pain."

To my horror she stood by the side of my bed, in her impeccable starched uniform and mask, looking scared stiff.

"Oh no," she said. "You must try to hold it back—I would rather wait for the doctor."

Then *I* was frightened. I knew I could give birth myself all right, but suppose she really was too nervous to do what was necessary, suppose she let something go wrong with my baby? Against all my instincts, miserably, I struggled hard to fight against the pains, and I found it far more painful and exhausting than giving birth. By the time the doctor came, the pains seemed to have lost their force, and I didn't seem to have any strength left for them anyway. The baby's birth was conscious hard work, instead of the joyous experience of my two previous confinements.

But Helen was born at last, although when she arrived the doctor had to hold her up by the feet and smack her bottom before she would cry; and nothing mattered, once I had her in my arms. With the doctor's consent, I got rid of the nurse after two weeks, and looked after Helen myself from then.

And so I completed the first part of my family.

6

Toxaemia

The four children were growing up, when I started Christopher; and Victoria, who shares my feeling about babies, was longing for his arrival as much as I was. As I had never had any complications with any of my previous pregnancies, I didn't expect any; and all went normally until a month before Christopher was due.

I had just had my monthly examination, and everything had been in order. The next day, when I was sitting darning socks and listening to the wireless with Steven after lunch, I glanced down and it seemed to me there was something odd about my feet.

"Steven," I said, "didn't I once have ankles?"

Steven came and had a look. "Yes, they don't usually look like that," he said. "They're all swollen."

I couldn't see them very clearly past the bulge in front of me, but it was obvious enough that he was right.

I telephoned the doctor. He came, looked at my ankles, took my blood pressure, looked concerned, and ordered me to bed at once.

"But what's wrong?" I wanted to know.

"I'm afraid, toxaemia," he said.

I'd never heard of it.

"We used to call it pre-eclampsia," he explained helpfully.

I'd never heard of that either.

"Well, it may be all right, if you rest," he said. "But you must stay in bed now until the baby's born. The danger is that there may be damage to the kidneys, and then it would be serious. You might go into a coma, or have an eclamptic fit."

"But I'm not ill!" I protested.

But apparently I was.

The doctor explained that it is not known what causes the kidneys to break down during pregnancy, but if they do, there is no known cure, except the immediate birth of the baby.

Two days later tests confirmed that my condition was serious. Although I still felt exactly the same as I had before I noticed my ankles, and I was not suffering from any of the other outward symptoms, I had in fact serious toxaemia, and was likely, the doctor told me, to die at any moment if the baby wasn't born at once; and I was rushed into hospital to have the birth brought on by a surgical induction.

By then I was in a state of terror in no way relieved by the fact that I continued to feel perfectly normal in health. I have always thought, and I still do, that hospitals are very bad places in which to have babies; and even worse places in which to lie waiting, wondering whether you and your baby are going to live or die. It was thirty-six hours after the induction before I started labour, and by then I was too miserable to care what happened, so long as it was soon over and I could know that my baby would live.

I started pains in the middle of the night, and they moved me into the labour ward a few hours later. There they gave me an injection of pethydine, and I fell into a heavy sleep. I awoke to the terrifying realization that I was lying in a totally strange place in the dark, and that I was going to have a baby in a very few minutes.

I felt for the bell in the dark and pressed it hard. The night sister came in, and ran out to telephone the specialist who was attending me. When she came back she said he was on his way.

"But the baby's coming *now*!" I said frantically.

"Well—try to hold it back," she said. "I can't give you an anaesthetic, only a doctor can do that, and there isn't a doctor on duty just now."

"Can't I have gas and air?" I asked.

"No, not with toxaemia," she said.

She started pushing the bed forward.

"What are you doing?" I asked.

"Getting the bed into position for the doctor to give an anaesthetic when he comes."

"But I can't wait," I cried.

"Well—perhaps you'd better have gas and air," she said, handing me the mask. "Now, breathe deeply and try to hold back—the doctor will be here before the next pain comes."

Suddenly I was more angry than frightened, angry at the unreality and frustration surrounding what should have been a natural and straightforward process.

I lifted my face out of the mask and said shortly, "He can't—it's here now," and then I turned on my back and pushed with all my strength—and Christopher was born.

I don't think the sister realized what I was doing until he landed on the bed, and cried.

I sat up and said, "Oh, that's wonderful," conscious of the most tremendous physical and mental relief I had ever experienced.

The sister cut the cord, wrapped him in a blanket, still damp, and put him into my arms. He was very tiny—only five and a half pounds—but he looked straight into my eyes as if with recognition, and his eyes were as blue as a June sky. I kissed his face, and wondered how it is that however many babies you have, the newest born is always the only baby you have ever known.

A few minutes later the specialist walked in. I noticed with some indignation that he was freshly shaved—so that's what he'd been doing when the sister said he was "on the way!"

"You're a bit late, aren't you?" I said, with Christopher in my arms.

He agreed he was.

The sister took Christopher again, and I asked for a glass of water. I learned later that I had a temperature of 101 all that night, so perhaps it wasn't surprising that I felt a bit odd.

There was no one else to do it, so the specialist brought me the water. He handed it to me courteously—the only thing he had done for me so far—and I took it from him, sitting on the hard bed of the labour ward, naked from the waist down, feeling for the first time that even near-tragedy had its funny side.

After it was over, my one idea was to get out of hospital. Times had changed since I had my last baby—I was allowed to get out of bed on the third day. The toxaemia was over, and I felt perfectly fit;

but they kept finding reasons why I ought to stay a little longer, until I felt that I should soon be turned into a chronic invalid.

I was trying to feed Christopher, but he was so small and sleepy the moment they brought him to me to feed he fell asleep, and I hadn't the heart to keep waking him up to suck. The nurses got cross, both with him and me, and said if I only cuddled him he would never feed; and I said he would feed when he was ready, and he needed cuddling as much as feeding—and he was my baby anyway.

They insisted on patting him and shaking him to try to keep him awake; and then one nurse slapped him, quite hard, and made him cry; and that made me cry, and it seemed to me it was all very bad for both of us.

I was quite sure everything would be all right if only I could get out of hospital; and in the end the specialist agreed, and let me take Christopher home on the tenth day.

Our home-coming was a wonderful moment. The children had been longing to see the baby: Geoffrey just stood and gazed at him with adoration in his face; Steven and Helen clustered round wanting to touch and kiss him; and I took him to Victoria and told her to sit in the biggest chair, and laid him in her arms. She sat there holding him, her bright gold head bent over his little face, her eyes intent and shining, looking like the Virgin Mary in a Christmas tableau.

His first bath, the day after we came home, was a most exciting affair. I had never handled a baby so small, and the children had never seen one; they all helped, and after we had finished and Christopher was sucking contentedly, the district nurse arrived to bath him, as I had left hospital before two weeks were up; and was rather surprised to find it already done. Steven, Helen and Victoria were all even anxious to do his washing!

After Christopher's birth, the specialist warned me that I ought not to risk having another baby. But I wanted one so badly, and it did appear that there was no certain danger involved; and as I pointed out to the specialist, it seemed to me I had only had trouble with Christopher not because I had had so many babies but because I had been out of practice.

When, three months after Christopher's birth, I knew Nicholas

Geoffrey digging a path
through the snow

Steven cycling through the water-splash

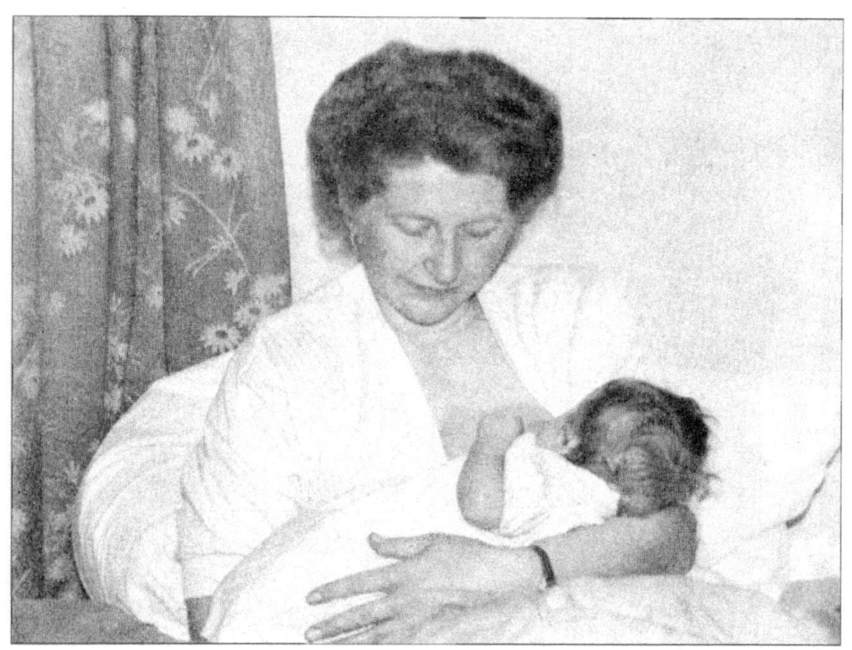

The author with Carol

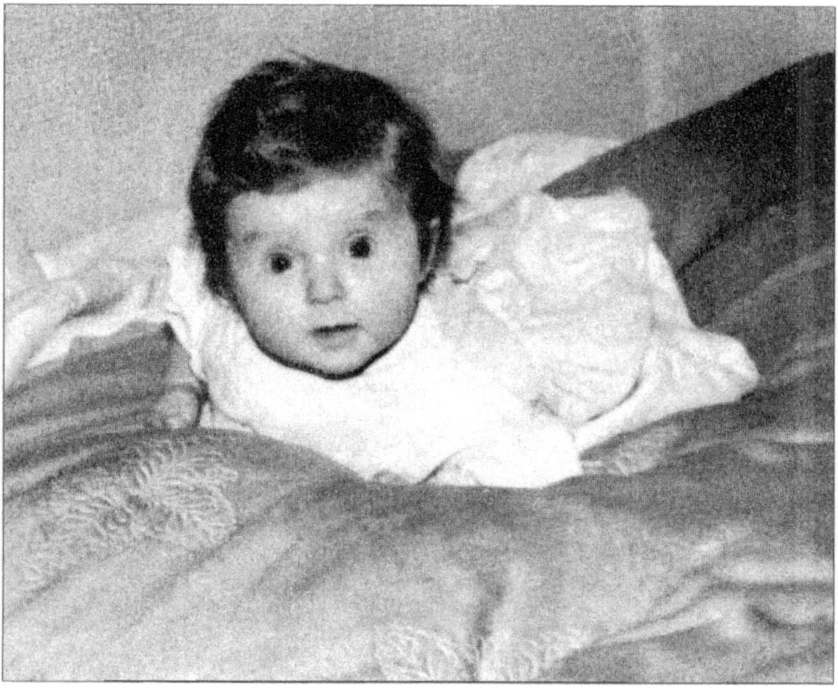

Carol--one month old

was on the way, my doctor was horrified, and maintained that I could not possibly have another without having serious trouble with toxaemia, that I would have to go into hospital for at least three months before the baby was due anyway, and in his opinion I ought to have the pregnancy terminated.

However, three months later I saw the specialist again, and he was less gloomy, and merely advised sufficient rest and ordinary care.

I carried Nicholas without incident until a week before he was due to be born; then my blood pressure went up and the doctor diagnosed slight toxaemia, and decided that it would be advisable to avoid trouble by performing another induction. Reluctantly I went into hospital, leaving Victoria to look after Christopher; by then she was quite able to take charge of him single-handed.

The induction was carried out at eight o'clock in the morning, and nothing happened until two days later, when I was awakened by sharp, irregular pains, unlike any I had ever had before. After an hour of these I told the nurses I was ready to go into the labour ward, and they moved me in, but saying that I was going to have a long wait on a hard bed.

The pains grew worse—so bad that I found them difficult to bear. I was increasingly sure that these were second-stage pains, and that the baby was ready to be born; it seemed to me that I must have had the first stage before I woke up, or not at all. But when I told the sister in charge this she said no, and I mustn't push yet, and left me alone before I could argue.

The pains mounted steadily, and I grew frightened. A nurse came in with my morning post. Never have I wanted to read letters less.

"Sister says you've got a long time to wait yet," she said brightly.

"Tell sister she isn't lying where I am," I said.

Then there came a pain that there was no resisting; my body pushed without any effort from me. I put my finger on the bell and kept it there until sister came.

"I can't *help* pushing," I said.

She walked round the bed and had a look, and I saw her eyebrows go up.

"Yes, well, the baby's head is showing," she said. "I'm afraid the specialist is away today—we couldn't catch him in time before he left—but there is another doctor in the hospital who could come if you like."

"I don't want a doctor," I said.

I turned over on to my back and pushed hard, and Nicholas was born. It was just two hours since I came into the labour ward, three hours since I'd started having pains—the shortest and most painful labour I'd ever had.

"I thought you said I had a long time to wait?" I said.

"Well—they do come on quickly sometimes."

I didn't like to point out that that was what I had been trying to tell her for two hours past.

I was back in bed again by the time the specialist got in, and came to see me. As soon as he came through the door of the ward I said, "When can I go home?"

"We'll let you go as soon as you've been on your feet if you like—in three days," he said.

So I took Nicholas home only three days old, in an ambulance. When we reached the house the attendants carried me in, but they didn't think they could get the stretcher up the stairs, so they laid it, and me, down on the kitchen floor while they considered the matter. I didn't think much of lying there waiting, so I quietly got up and walked upstairs to my bedroom, where my husband had already taken Nicholas and laid him in his cradle.

"I made his cradle up," Victoria told me, "and I aired everything." She stood by the cradle proudly. "And I looked after Christopher all the time you were in hospital, and he's quite all right. He cried a little at night, so I took him into my room. I think he's got another tooth through. Do you want to see him now?"

She carried Christopher in, and I sat on the bed and put my arms round all five of them. Nicholas lay in the cradle peacefully sleeping. It was so lovely to be home.

7

The Weenybedes

It was Victoria who invented the name. While I was carrying Christopher, three of our cats had kittens, and we kept one of each; they grew up together, and became Victoria's special care; and for some reason that she was never able to explain, she called them the Weenybedes. When Christopher was born, the name became transferred to him; and our babies have been known as the weenybedes ever since.

When Christopher was three months old, I had a very painful infection of one finger, and had to have the nail removed from the first finger of my right hand. For weeks afterwards, it had to be kept bandaged, and I could not put it into water. Victoria became, literally, my right hand instead. When I bathed Christopher, I soaped him, and she helped me to lift him into the water; I supported his head with my left hand, and she sponged him and helped me lift him out. She did all his washing, and helped me change and dress him, using both of her hands with the remaining one of mine. By the time my nail had grown again, she could bath and dress him by herself, her only difficulty being that at first her lap wasn't big enough to hold him comfortably; but she sat in a big chair, and it was helpful that he was a very small baby.

'How did you learn to look after us?' she wanted to know.

When I had Geoffrey I hadn't known anything about babies; I had to find it out by myself. He was a very good baby, and I had managed quite well until it came to weaning him. Unlike most babies, he had a positive horror of putting anything in his mouth— and this included food. As soon as I put a spoonful of cereal in, he put it out; a messy and depressing process that quite often left us both in tears. I often think now how reassuring it would have been if I could have seen ahead then to his present capacity for roast beef and batter pudding and rounds of bread about an inch thick. At the time I often wondered frantically if he ever *would* take solid food! Even Steven, who was comparatively much easier, for a long time would not take anything unless it was well sugared—including things like beef broth and carrots.

Victoria and I weaned Christopher together, and we all thoroughly enjoyed it. Certainly he was a very good baby, but I am convinced that a great measure of success in weaning depends on taking the attitude that it doesn't really matter whether the child eats or not. This is a difficult attitude for an anxious mother, although it comes easier when you have reared a number of children already; but, I soon realized, it is easiest of all for another child. Feeding Christopher was a game for Victoria, much more interesting than playing with dolls, and the fact that she looked forward to it ensured Christopher's enjoying it too.

Very much the same thing applied to 'potting'. I have never believed in early pot training; the waste of time and irritation caused by holding a small baby out seems to me to be damaging to the nerves of both mother and child. I much prefer washing nappies. But even a late start involves a certain amount of patience; there can be nothing more frustrating to a small child than sitting on its pot with an adult standing over it obviously expecting something which the child may or may not be ready at that time to produce. We got Christopher his first pot when he was a year old, and Victoria and I carefully sat him on it and strapped him comfortably to the leg of the nursery chair. Then I left Victoria with him while I got on with cooking our breakfast. Christopher considered the matter, carefully twisted himself round until he had his back to her—and did all that was required of him in about three minutes. When we came to the House on the Hill, he was still having wet nappies, but anything else was an accident, and Victoria was able to say proudly that she had trained him herself.

Now it was summer; our first summer at the House on the Hill, and one of the hottest we had ever known. Our days were full;

with the house to run, the weenybedes to look after, the garden to establish, and my baby increasingly on the way.

Victoria and I weaned Nicholas, and he was as good as Christopher, with one exception. Periodically, he got the idea of blowing as soon as I put a mouthful in. The only way to overcome this, I discovered, was to make noises, all through his feed, which could be made with a closed mouth; and he would copy them throughout the meal. But if I opened my mouth to speak or laugh, he opened his—and blew. So feeding Nicholas involved my saying 'Mmm-mmm! Mmmmm!' the whole time, and sounding like a cow talking to its calf, with Nicholas going 'Mmmmmm!' back to me. But there were still some days when, however much I moo'd, Nicholas laughed—and blew. It is difficult not to get irritated when you are being covered in sticky cereal; but if Nicholas thought that I was cross, he started to cry, which was worse. So when he started blowing again, I handed him over to Victoria, and she fed him without the slightest difficulty. After all, when you are nine and a half, it is quite possible to be amused and not exasperated at having a mouthful of spinach blown suddenly into your face.

I have never believed in prams, feeling that a baby sleeps better in a cot by an open window in a quiet room, than outside in the changing vagaries of the weather. But we got Christopher a push-chair as soon as he could sit up, and every afternoon one of us took him for a walk.

His usual immediate reaction, as soon as the push-chair started moving, was to fall asleep. This he refused to do leaning back on a pillow, but slept bending forward, his face resting on his hands on the metal rim of the chair. When the sun was very hot I was afraid of the resulting exposure of the back of his neck, so we used to pick a large dock leaf from the roadside and tuck it into the back of his collar. The general effect was odd, but the result was satisfactory.

The only thing that would wake him before he had finished his sleep was the passing of a farm tractor. Like Geoffrey, he was obviously going to be a farmer when he grew up. As the sound approached, up came the little drooping head, and sleepy blue eyes opened to watch it pass—then his eyelashes fell again, the golden head drooped, and he was again asleep. People who passed us grew quite used to the sight of the curls on the back of Christopher's head—it was only occasionally that anyone saw his face.

When harvest time came, Victoria and I took him to the harvest fields, where he could watch the binders and combines at work. The first time he saw a combine he couldn't take his eyes off it, and obviously wanted to take it home with him. He stood up in his chair and gazed, and held out his hands for it, and cried when we had to take him back.

Soon he was learning to walk, and our expeditions became accordingly slower; we had to let him get out of the chair and toddle beside it at least part of the way. He was a very tidy child, and his walks were slowed down still more by his insistence on picking up every tiny stone he could see on the road, and giving it to Victoria or me to throw away before we went on.

One evening when we had come back from our walk and Victoria was giving Christopher his tea, she called to me excitedly— "Look! He's feeding himself!"

He had picked up his mug and was drinking out of it, holding it firmly with both hands. We watched, fascinated; but when he put the mug down, still half-full, neither of us was quick enough to anticipate his next move. Suddenly he turned the mug upside down over the tray of his high chair. Then, before Victoria or I could do it, he proceeded to wipe up the spilt milk carefully with his feeder.

Nicholas also was growing rapidly. He was chubby, in rolls of fat all over, with firm little hands that had surprising strength. Geoffrey called him the Little Blacksmith.

Soon we started putting him on the floor. He couldn't crawl, but if there was something in sight that he wanted, he rolled, wriggled, and pushed himself forward until he got to it. Christopher started taking an interest in him, but he was disconcerted when he offered Nicholas his toys—a firm little hand came out and grabbed, and Christopher turned to us with an appealing face, wondering how the toy had gone. But he began to show a very real affection for Nicholas all the same, and put his arms round him when he found him on the floor, and went on bringing him toys.

Outside the weenybedes' bedroom window was a pear tree, and this had always fascinated Christopher, who loved watching the movement of the leaves swaying in wind or rain. Now Nicholas started watching it too. Every night when we tucked them up in their cots, they would lie listening to the rustle of the thick leaves, where pears were steadily ripening.

Victoria and I made up the Weenybedes' Lullaby about it, and every evening we sang to them in their baths:

Hushabye, rockabye, hushabye wee,

Rockabye, Weenybedes, in your pear tree.

When it grew dark the moon came up behind the pear tree, and threw a silvery light all over their room. Fair curls and dark curls over their pillows, eyes closed, and little hands thrown over their heads, Christopher and Nicholas slept.

8

Keeping Dry

One Sunday morning in the hottest part of the summer, I came downstairs as usual and took the kettle to fill it for early morning tea. I pumped for several minutes, but nothing came out. This had happened before, so I called to Steven to come and prime the pump with a jug of water, and got on with preparing the weenybedes' breakfast. Steven poured water in and pumped for some time, with no result.

"There's nothing coming up at all," he reported. "The well must have gone dry."

Of course it would happen on a Sunday—these things always do. We had the weenybedes' clothes and nappies to wash, the dinner to cook—and not even drinking water in the house, Steven having used the reserve jug, which we kept for emergencies, to prime the pump. As soon as we had finished breakfast, I sent Geoffrey down to get a bucket of water from our nearest neighbours at the bottom of the hill, and began to consider how to deal with the rest of the position.

Being a dry spell, of course our soft water butts were empty too. I wondered about the derelict cottages—they must have a well. I took a bucket and a length of rope, and went to see.

They had—an equally derelict well, the top of it broken and fallen in—but when I pulled the boards away and looked, there *was* water about six feet down. The problem was how to get it out.

I lowered my bucket on the rope. When it reached the water, it floated. Bending precariously over the edge, I did everything I could think of to sink it, but obstinately it remained afloat. I had an idea that there was some knack in dropping a bucket into a well so that it went under, but I didn't know what it was, so that was no help. I gave up, and hunted round for a long stick. Finding a suitable one in the hedge, I returned with it to the well.

Manipulating the bucket with one hand, and the stick with the other, I pushed and pulled until I got the bucket on to its side in the water. Slowly it filled up. Straightening it carefully, I pulled it up again, spilling a good deal of water in the process, and carried it back. By the time I reached the house again it had taken me more than twenty minutes to get just over half a bucket of water. Obviously we had to think of something else.

I turned my attention to the pond. It was at any rate considerably nearer to the house. Like most farm ponds, it was irregular in shape, with its edges varying from steep banks to sloping muddy shallows. Fortunately the cattle and horses had been taken off that field some weeks before, so the water was fairly clean and undisturbed. The question again was how to get at it.

After I had explored all round the edge I decided that the back of the pond, where a shelved bank sloped down to a deep clear pool, was the most practicable. By then Geoffrey was back with a bucket of clean water, so he and Steven and I took another bucket to the pond. Steven climbed down the bank, holding the bucket in one hand; when he reached the water Geoffrey leaned down and gripped his free hand, while Steven lowered the bucket into the water with the other. Then Geoffrey helped Steven to lift the full bucket up to the top of the bank, and they took turns to bring the buckets back to the house.

We filled the copper, and started cooking dinner while it heated; then Geoffrey and Steven went on bringing buckets of cold water, while Victoria and I did the washing. There was a certain amount of weed in the water, as well as dead leaves, and there may even have been a few small fishes—but we got the washing out on the line.

The next morning I telephoned the builder who had fitted the pump to the well. He came and climbed down the well, and reported that there was plenty of water there, but the pipe from the pump wasn't long enough to reach it—he had to extend it by another fifteen feet.

He scratched his head in some perplexity.

"That well was full right up to the top when I put the pump in," he said. "You must have used *hundreds* of gallons of water!"

I said I thought that was quite likely.

"There's all the weenybedes' washing," explained Victoria.

One very hot afternoon not long after this, Steven and I had been gardening, clearing the weeds from one of the still unused flower beds. We were finding it very hot work. Steven dug with enthusiasm on the first half of the bed, he with the spade and I with the fork; then we changed over and I did the spadework.

After a time Steven said, "It's easier going this end, isn't it?"

I looked up in some surprise, perspiration running down my face—and saw him leaning comfortably on the fork, in the shade of an apple tree.

"That depends," I suggested, "on the position you're in."

Steven looked guilty, and said it was too hot to dig.

"All right," I said. "Is it too hot for you to go to the village and get ice creams for everyone?"

He said it wasn't. So he went off on his bicycle; and as no one else felt like moving, I told him I would come to meet him, and went in to get Christopher ready for his walk.

By the time we had reached the bottom of the field, Christopher was asleep. I had forgotten to bring the pillow we usually carried to put under his face on the metal rim of the chair; I couldn't let him be bumped on it all the way down the road, and I was too tired to go back. At the bottom of the drift there was a gateway opening into another field, and a patch of soft grass in the opening, under the shade of an elder tree. Carefully I lifted the sleeping Christopher, sat down on the grass, and laid him on my skirt. Then I lay back, one arm across him—and in a little while I also fell asleep.

Steven woke us when he came back with the ices. Christopher sat up in surprise and said "Der!" The others had come down the field to meet Steven, so we all sat down on the grass and ate our ices in the shade.

By the time we had finished we were cooler, so Victoria said she would go and get the weenybedes' tea, while Steven came with me to finish Christopher's walk.

"Where shall we go?" I asked Steven.

"To the water-splash," he said.

The water-splash was a stream that runs under the road about half a mile away, making a pool each side—and in bad weather, right across the road as well. Now it was reduced to a shallow trickle of water on either side.

We found it deserted, and climbing through the railings, sat on the grass, took our sandals off, and paddled our feet in the water.

Christopher said, "Der, der, der!" in great excitement, and bounced up and down in his chair.

"Can't he paddle, too?" asked Steven.

"I don't see why not," I said.

We took his sandals off and gently lifted him in. At first he pulled his feet up as soon as they touched the cool water, but after a few minutes he let us stand him in the stream while we held his hands. When he got tired we lifted him back into his chair and dried his feet on my handkerchief, and Steven and I sat and threw stones into the water, so he could watch them splash.

Steven said, "I met the roadman when I was going to get the ices. He says there's a baby show in the village next week, and we ought to put Christopher in it."

The roadman had got to know Christopher on our afternoon walks.

When we got back to the house, we told Victoria.

"Oh, *can* we?" she cried. "And Nicholas too?"

"I'd like to," I said, "but where are they having the baby show?"

"At the Vicarage," Steven said.

The Vicarage is at least two miles from our hill.

"How could we get them both there?" I wanted to know. "I can't carry Nicholas all that way in my arms, and we've only got Christopher's push-chair."

"Couldn't I carry Nicholas?" asked Geoffrey.

"I don't think so, not four miles, and you'd have to hold him all the time we were there," I said.

"Couldn't we take them both in the barrow?" suggested Helen.

I didn't think that would be really satisfactory. Then I had a sudden idea.

"Victoria, couldn't we take Nicholas in your doll's pram?"

Victoria hadn't played with dolls since she had the weenybedes.

"Oh, yes!" she said. "But could we get him into it?"

"We could try," I said.

So we got the pram out and cleaned it and put in cushions, and laid Nicholas carefully inside. He fitted in exactly, and laughed with delight.

So, a week later, we set off for the Vicarage. Geoffrey cycled ahead, as I wanted him to do some shopping for me, and also to find out exactly where we had to go; Victoria pushed Nicholas, and Steven pushed Christopher, and Helen carried a basket containing a change of nappies and a comb and brush, while I walked alongside like a swan with a brood of cygnets.

It was a very hot, thundery day, with heavy clouds on the horizon. Both the babies fell asleep before we got there, but they woke up as we went through the gate. We were only just in time, and leaving Helen and Steven with Geoffrey, who was waiting for us at the entrance, Victoria and I joined a procession of mothers with prams making their way to the Vicarage lawn.

The woman in charge came up to us.

"How old is he?"

"I'm entering two," I said.

"Two?" She looked, startled, at Victoria and the doll's pram. I lifted Nicholas out.

She took details of both of them. Then Victoria lifted Christopher out of his chair, and we carried them both into the Vicarage drawing-room.

It was crowded. Victoria and I found a quiet corner, and since all the chairs were already occupied, sat down with the babies on the floor. Christopher sat down, took one of his sandals off, and proceeded to examine it, oblivious of everybody. Nicholas looked a little apprehensive.

All went well until the doctor came round. First, a lady I didn't know came and looked at the babies, and exclaimed over my double entry. Nicholas approved of her, and both he and Christopher gazed at her with wide blue eyes.

Then the doctor came to look at them. Christopher remained unperturbed, and interested only in his sandal. But Nicholas took one look—and burst into tears. I soothed and comforted him, but it was no use. After the doctor had gone on, he stopped crying and buried his face in my shoulder. Then he cautiously lifted his head again, looked round, saw the doctor a few feet away examining the next baby—and with an expression of absolute horror, burst into tears again.

The doctor turned round and regarded him doubtfully.

"I don't think he likes me," he said.

We all sat in suspense waiting for the result of the judging. Christopher was beaten in his class by a stolid little boy who was standing throughout the proceedings; Christopher preferred to sit, although perfectly well able to stand. But Nicholas won a prize.

We all went out again, and found the others waiting for us on the lawn. The prizes were presented by the lady who had helped with the judging. Handing me and Nicholas ours, she said smilingly, "I think he deserved it!"

I went back to the children and started to open the wrapping.

"What is it?" said Helen.

"Wasn't there something you wanted me to get from the village while we were here?" asked Geoffrey. "The shops will be shut soon."

"Well, yes, there was," I said. "But you won't have to now. Nicholas has got it for us."

His prize was a cake of baby soap and a tin of baby powder!

All this time the thunder clouds had been steadily moving up the sky. Now a few drops of rain began to fall, and everyone began gathering up their belongings in a hurry. Gathering up all my belongings was quite a job, but we hastily fitted Nicholas back into his pram, put Christopher into his chair, and set off for home, Geoffrey cycling ahead to collect mackintoshes in case we needed them.

We hadn't gone more than a few hundred yards before the clouds opened, and the rain poured down. We pulled up the pram hood and apron over Nicholas, and I wrapped my jacket round

Christopher; but Steven, Helen, Victoria and I were getting soaked through.

Suddenly we saw the milk van coming towards us through the driving rain. The driver slowed down, and called out, "Do you want a lift home?"

"But you're going the other way!" I said.

"I'll turn round," he replied cheerfully. "Won't take long to run you back."

So we all climbed into the back of the van, lifting in the weenybedes still in their pram and chair, and we sat there among the empty milk bottles, while the van rattled along the wet road.

At the end of our drift it stopped, but only while the driver got out and took our crate of milk, which he had left in our barrow only half an hour previously, on board the van again.

"Keep inside!" he said. "I'll take you up to the house."

So we bumped over the rough track, across the field, and stopped at our garden gate. We climbed out, and lifted the weenybedes down.

"Thank you *very* much!" I said.

We all got out of our wet things, and when Geoffrey arrived on his bicycle a little later, Victoria and I were starting to get the weenybedes' tea. He was very surprised to find us all there.

"However did you get back?" he asked.

"Oh," I said, "we came home with the milk!"

9

Speed the Plough

Now summer gave way to autumn—and autumn gave way to tears. It rained and rained, and our field became muddier and muddier. A stream appeared, running across the bottom of our drift where it joined the road; the water spread higher and higher until all the bottom of the drift was under water. We splashed through it to fetch the milk and bread, and Christopher paddled in it, and the tradesmen who did bring goods to our door took to keeping rubber boots in their vans and changing into them before walking up.

People started saying to us, "But you're not going to stay here through the winter, surely?"—and as time went on, it became obvious that even if we *had* wanted to leave, the difficulty would have been getting out. We had mud up to our doorstep—and beyond. Our carpets and linoleum, however hard and often they were brushed and scrubbed, began to take on an earthy brown tint in place of their original colour.

"Anyway," said Geoffrey cheerfully, "the well won't run dry now!"

At the same time, Steven and I were busy planting shrubs and bulbs in the garden. Puddling about in mud, we dug holes with a spade heavy with sticky clay, and put in forsythia, flowering currant, lilac and almond and cherry trees—now only bare brown twigs—and thought of the far-off spring.

Rain dripped off the apple trees down the backs of our necks as we straightened up after each hole.

"Do we have to carry out the instructions they send with the trees?" Steven wanted to know.

"Why?"

"Well, it says 'water thoroughly immediately after planting'!"

We planted daffodils in the grass under the apple trees, and bluebells in the old rubbish dump after the nasturtiums had died. We filled the flower beds with tulips and narcissi and wallflowers and forget-me-nots and roses; and then sat indoors watching them being thoroughly watered after planting, while we drank our tea.

Every batch of shrubs that arrived seemed a bit harder to dig holes for, as the ground got heavier and I got bigger.

My figure grew steadily more noticeable, and I began to think of all the things about the place that needed doing before winter and the baby came, that we had put off doing during the long summer days.

"Geoffrey," I said at breakfast one damp, tawny morning, "I want you to do a few repairs."

"What?" asked Geoffrey.

"Well," I said, "there's the broken window in Helen's bedroom—we shall have to fix Windolite over that—and the catch on Victoria's window needs replacing; the gutters have got grass growing in them, you'll have to borrow a ladder and clean them out with a trowel; and the water butts need cleaning out too before the next downpour; the oil stoves need new wicks fitted, and that hole in the ceiling over Steven's bed needs covering somehow, bits off the roof keep falling through; the apples must be gathered, when you've got the ladder, and then you'll have to clean out the shed—Steven and the girls can help with that—and make a place to store them."

"All right, all right!" said Geoffrey, as I paused for breath. "What do you want me to do *first?*"

"Better clean the gutters," I said, "and then the water butts..." And before I could go through it all again, Geoffrey got up and went out to borrow a ladder.

He came back with the ladder and called to me from the kitchen door.

"I've just seen our landlord," he said. "He says he's going to plough up three of the fields up here, and put in wheat—the small field at the back of the house, the field up the loke, and our field in front."

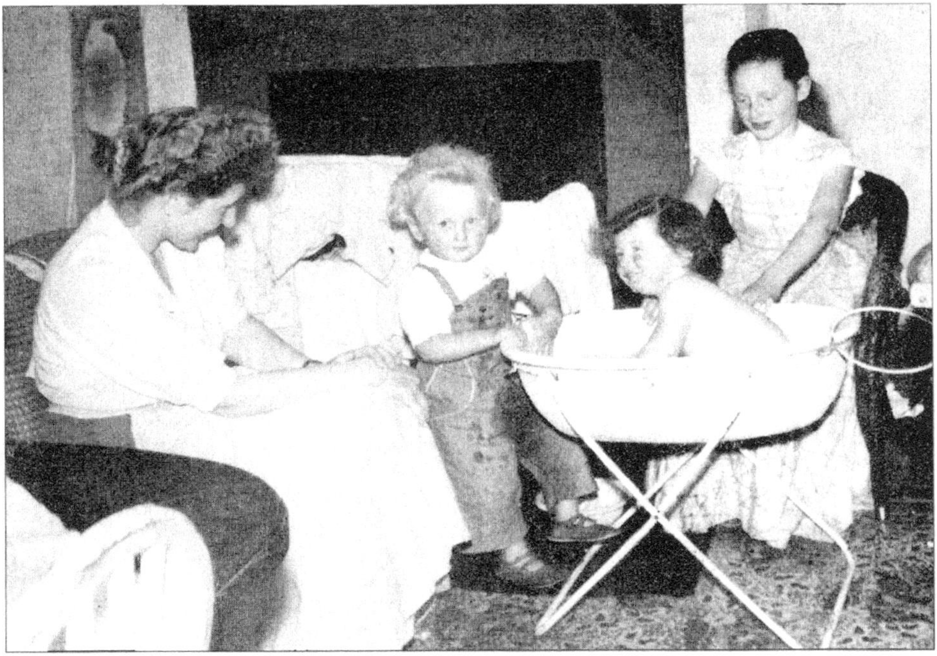

Bath time for Christopher and Nicholas

Helen and Nicholas

Nicholas with the washing-bowl

Victoria with Danilo

Christopher and Nicholas
with the rabbits

Geoffrey with the sheep

Christopher with his tricycle

"Will they take the horses and cows away, then?" asked Victoria.

"No," said Geoffrey. "I asked him, and they're putting the cows on the big field, and the horses on the field at the top of the loke."

"But what about our track?" I wanted to know.

"He says he'll put that back after the field's drilled," said Geoffrey.

"Until then I suppose we stay in, cut off from the mainland," I said quite cheerfully. "When are they going to start?"

"Tomorrow morning—or today, if they can get round to it," replied Geoffrey, now halfway up the ladder. "This doesn't feel very steady. Can Steven come and stand on the bottom rung to stop it wobbling?"

Steven went out to help, and Victoria and I got on with the washing and washing-up.

About mid-afternoon we heard a tractor coming up the drift.

"They're going to start on the field at the back," Geoffrey reported.

"Can I go and watch?" said Helen.

For several days after that, we heard the undulating roar of the tractor engine up and down the back fields, and Helen came in reluctantly for meals, her face streaked with mud and tractor grease; but our field was left undisturbed. And still it rained.

And then one morning we heard the roar approaching steadily, closer and closer, until it was under our windows. We all rushed to look out. The tractor and plough drove steadily across the wet green grass of our field, leaving a track of new brown earth behind them.

I didn't go out that day until mid-afternoon, when I went down the field to fetch the milk. Then I found, barring my way, a strip of rough brown earth clods, cutting across our track. I picked my way over it carefully and hoped they would get it put back before I had to go down the field again.

The next day the ploughing was finished.

"When are they going to drill it?" I asked Geoffrey.

"Tomorrow," he said, "as soon as they've harrowed it."

The back fields were harrowed and drilled already.

That night it rained. It came down in buckets—a downpour and a flood. By the morning our garden was a series of pools, and the field a lake with brown islands, where big clods of earth stuck up here and there. I looked at it in horror.

"The field's under flood!" I called to the family. "We're marooned!"

Gradually the water subsided, but the heavy clay soil was left soaked and sticky. And still it rained.

We had to get across the field to fetch up our milk and bread. Walking over it was a difficult and laborious job. Our feet slipped and slithered and stuck, and my steadily increasing weight made the crossing a feat of balance and endurance.

On the second day, Steven woke up with bad toothache. He was in so much pain that I told Geoffrey to get to the telephone and make an appointment with the dentist as early as possible. He set off down the field, and returned to say that the dentist could see Steven that afternoon.

It was a cold, misty day. Trains and buses being infrequent, we had to cycle into the town, five miles away. We started off, Geoffrey helping me, half pushing, half carrying our bicycles down the field. When we got to the dentist, we found Steven's tooth was abscessed, and had to be taken out. The dentist warned me to be careful not to let him catch cold in it afterwards, and as he had no scarf, I took the tie off my fur-fabric coat and gave it to Steven to wrap round his mouth.

We had a long, cold ride home in the gathering dusk. It was quite dark when we reached the drift, and too misty to see the lights of the house. We started dragging our bicycles up the field. The wheels clogged up with mud, and we couldn't see where we were going. Soon it became impossible to move them any further, and I began to feel that I couldn't move any further too. I shouted—Steven couldn't open his mouth—feeling like an explorer lost in a trackless bog a hundred miles from civilization.

I told Steven to go on ahead, leaving his bicycle in the mud, and I leaned on mine and tried not to panic. After what seemed like hours, I saw a light flickering dimly ahead. Then I heard Geoffrey's voice shouting, "Where are you?" He reached me and helped me up the rest of the way.

When we reached the house I joined Steven by the fire, both

of us nearly exhausted. There remained our bicycles, abandoned in the field. Victoria and Helen put on boots and went out with Geoffrey, and together they managed to find them and bring them in. They were so clogged with mud that the wheels would no longer go round.

After that, Geoffrey and Steven carried all our bicycles down the field, in daylight, cleaned the mud out of them, and left them leaning against an old wagon abandoned near our safe on the roadside, covering them with an old mackintosh. They could at least then be used when needed, without the difficulty of transporting them across the field each time.

No tradesmen could now get up to the house. Our safe wasn't big enough to accommodate everything that we needed delivered. Paraffin, our most heavy necessity, and the most important, presented our biggest problem. Geoffrey and Steven managed to get our garden barrow down the field, and walked to the village shop with it, taking a five-gallon paraffin can. They brought the barrow back and somehow managed to get it up the field again, loaded with groceries and the five gallons of paraffin.

"Perhaps it would be easier if it rained a bit more," suggested Geoffrey, as they struggled up the field. "We might be able to get up and down by boat."

Then there came a pause in the rain. For several days it was dry; the pools disappeared, the surface of the clay was only damp, and one morning we heard the welcome sound of the tractor approaching beneath our windows.

Slowly, with many halts when the tractor wheels got stuck, they got the field harrowed. It had only to be drilled, and harrowed again, and our track could be rolled and trodden down.

Anxiously we watched. The drilling started. At half past three one grey November afternoon, it was nearly done. Then the skies opened, and rain poured down. The tractor and drill went back to the farm.

It rained all night—it rained all the next day. The field was flooded again; the uncovered corn lay or floated in pools all over it. The wet, sticky earth squelched round our boots again, and we slid further than we walked across it. I sent Geoffrey urgently to the farm to ask what could be done.

The answer was, "Nothing." "The land's too wet and sticky to get the tractor over," Geoffrey reported. "They're afraid of getting it stuck."

"If only the rain had held off for another day!" said Steven.

"If only they'd got on quicker with it in the first place!" I said crossly. "I can't have a baby in the middle of a bog!"

But nothing could be done now. We had to reorganize our lives to deal with the existing conditions—with Christmas and the baby getting nearer every day. And still it rained.

Christopher and Nicholas could no longer be taken out in the push-chair; it was impossible to get it, or them, across the field. Our bicycles had to be permanently housed against the wagon by the roadside. Geoffrey and Steven continued to fetch our supplies from the village, by barrow, each week. Whenever we went out we had to squelch and slither over the trackless expanse of wet, slippery clay. When I went to see the doctor for my routine examination I told him that the field had been ploughed up, but he took it in his stride, and said it wouldn't be the first time he had had to visit a patient in rubber boots.

It was now only a few weeks to Christmas, and we had to deal with that as well as everything else. I went shopping, in the bigger town twenty miles away, in boots muddy up to the knee. Geoffrey went with me to carry parcels, which he carefully avoided examining too closely. Victoria looked after the weenybedes for the day, and Steven met us at the station when we returned—with the barrow.

We got in, by barrow, a supply of fuel and food to last us over the Christmas holiday, and Victoria, Steven and I spent one afternoon baking pastry. The larder and every available cupboard became full of enticing smells, and our cats showed a marked reluctance to move from the vicinity of the larder door. Our oldest tom cat, known as Big Large, established himself on top of what used to be a wall oven, and defied all our efforts to dislodge him; while his younger but even bigger rival, Big Huge, settled down on the top of the kitchen cabinet, from where he made dabs at us with one hopeful paw as we went on putting jam tarts, mince pies, and sausage rolls inside the cabinet.

A few days before Christmas we staggered home bringing the last of the parcels, and a Christmas tree as tall as ourselves. On Christmas Eve, while the girls and the weenybedes slept, Geoffrey, Steven and I decorated the tree, and Geoffrey and Steven hung paper chains and holly round the sitting room. Then, after they had gone to bed, I brought down all their presents and laid them in a pile at the foot of the tree.

When we lit the candles on the tree on Christmas morning, the house seemed to glow defiantly in its surrounding sea of mud. When Christopher came down to breakfast, he stood and gazed, spellbound, at the faerie world that had come into being while he slept.

And still it rained, all Christmas Day.

10

A Child is Born

With the coming of the New Year, the time of my baby's arrival drew very near. I was determined to have the baby at home, despite all difficulties. Each week I had visited the doctor, to be reassured each time—no sign of toxaemia, although my blood pressure was rather high, and the doctor kept telling me I should get more rest.

Gradually I handed over the running of the house to the four elder children. Geoffrey did all the shopping and business trips to the town, and all the heavy jobs about the house. Steven did the local shopping and took over most of the cooking, and he and Victoria shared the housework, while Victoria looked after Christopher and Nicholas. Helen did odd jobs and ran errands for everyone, and played with the weenybedes while Steven and Victoria worked. In the afternoons the children usually took it in turns to stay in the house while I lay down on the settee to rest, and Nicholas scuttled in his play-pen, Christopher ran round the room, and the others went out to play.

But one afternoon when Victoria and Helen were with the horses, and Steven and Geoffrey had taken the barrow to the village for supplies, I was alone in the house. I was lying on the settee, with Nicholas in his play-pen, and Christopher sitting beside me looking at a book upside-down, when there came a knock at the door. I heaved myself laboriously upright—I often thought that the effort of getting up when I had to outweighed the benefit of lying down in the first place—and went to answer it. Already halfway through the door was the doctor. He looked disturbed, and his feet were muddy.

I put Christopher, protesting, into the play-pen with Nicholas, and went upstairs.

After the routine examination, which he conducted in silence, the doctor sat down on my dressing-stool and fixed me with a determined eye.

"You will have to go into hospital to have this baby," he announced firmly.

"Why? What's wrong?" I asked, in panic.

"It's your seventh baby," he began portentously—"Yes, I know," I interrupted—"and you have a previous history of toxaemia…"

"Have I got it this time?"

"No," he said slowly, "there's nothing to worry about there so far, although your blood pressure is up, but that's understandable—but I think it is most inadvisable for you to have this baby at home."

"But why?" I broke in again, "if there's nothing wrong with me…"

"It is a question of parity," he declaimed. "You have had six children without trouble, except for the toxaemia, but a seventh baby is always regarded as most likely to cause complications, haemorrhage and so forth…"

"You mean," I said, feeling rather dazed, "I am likely to have complications with this baby because I didn't with any of the others…?"

"Well, not exactly, but there's always a risk…?"

"There's always a risk when I cross a road, or when the children climb a tree," I said, "but we don't all go and live in hospital on that account…"

The doctor got up and walked round the room. "How do you suppose we could get an ambulance up here?" he demanded.

"You couldn't," I agreed. "But I don't need an ambulance to have a baby."

"How are the nurse and I to get up here?"—he looked at his feet—"That field is in a frightful condition!"

"I know," I agreed again, "but I did tell you it had been ploughed up and you said it would be all right."

"I'd no idea it was as bad as this! You need only go into hospital for three days, if all goes well," he added persuasively, "then you could come home."

"How?" I asked. "If you can't get an ambulance up here, and the field is too bad for you to walk up, could I walk up it three days after having a baby? And if you mean you could carry me up on a stretcher, couldn't you equally well carry me down on a stretcher if anything does go wrong when the baby is born?"

"Now look," he said, "this isn't a fit place for a baby to be born, is it?"

"It will be its home, which is the right place for a baby to be born," I said. "And healthy babies have been born in far worse situations than this."

"Yes, but it isn't necessary now. Don't you think you ought to go into hospital and avoid all possible trouble?"

I took a deep breath.

"No," I said, "I don't. I'm sorry if it means that you and the nurse will have to walk up a muddy field, but I want to have my baby at home. And I don't think you ought to upset and frighten a woman in the last weeks of pregnancy. If I were a ewe in lamb you'd have the farmer after you."

"You're an obstinate woman," he said crossly, as he retreated down the stairs.

"So long as you can't diagnose anything worse than that," I retorted, "you shouldn't have anything to worry about."

When the children came in I was sitting on the settee with Christopher, feeling apprehensive about my condition for the first time.

"The doctor's been here," I told them. "He wants me to go into hospital to have the baby."

"Will you have to?" asked Victoria unhappily.

"What's wrong with you?" asked Geoffrey.

"No," I said firmly, "I'm *not* going to. There's nothing wrong, so far as I could gather. Nothing wrong with me, that is. There's only one thing he thought might be serious!"

"What?" demanded the four of them.

"Mud," I explained. "The muddy walk up the field."

Perhaps I was wrong in insisting on staying at the house with the field in the state it was. But I'd had two miserable hospital confinements, and I did so badly want to have this baby at home. And I did feel that if I could walk up and down the field almost every day when I was heavily pregnant, it should be possible for the doctor and nurse to do it a few times burdened with nothing more than a leather bag.

After this difference of opinion the doctor apparently accepted the position, and the nurse came to see me and arranged details about the confinement. I appealed urgently to our landlord to do something about providing a track to the house, and eventually he sent a horse and cartload of cinders, which he had spread all the way down the field, making the going slightly better, and we hoped that this would pacify the doctor and save his boots. Anyway it made it easier to get up and down with the barrow.

It was a Friday morning when I started the day feeling that something was going to happen, although I wasn't quite sure why. Victoria and I did the washing, I helped Steven get lunch into the oven, and then I became conscious of a faint pain in my back, that had been coming and going in a vague sort of way for the last half hour.

I went and lay down on the settee. When all the children were in for lunch, I said, "I think I've started labour."

"I'll go and telephone the doctor," said Geoffrey, and made for the door.

"Yes, I think you'd better," I said; "he told me to let him know as soon as I started, but there's no hurry. I'm only getting very slight pains, but they're regular, and I don't want any lunch. Tell him I've only just started labour, but I'm almost sure the baby is on the way."

Soon after the children finished lunch, the doctor arrived. His examination confirmed that labour had begun.

"I'll tell the nurse to come along this evening," he said as he left.

When he had gone I went upstairs and got into bed. It was dark when the nurse came, and Victoria had put the weenybedes in and settled them to sleep. The nurse started preparing for the baby's arrival.

"How long do you usually take?" she asked.

"About six hours, and then it comes with a rush," I said.

But the night went on, and nothing happened. The children

went to bed, and the nurse sat down to wait. I drifted in a haze of sleepiness, while the faint pains came and went, and I was conscious of a stirring within me, hard to define and impossible to explain, which I knew meant the baby was waiting to be born.

"I don't believe you're in labour at all!" the nurse said, quite crossly, at about three o'clock in the morning.

"I can't help it," I said.

I began to feel very hot, although the nurse said I hadn't a temperature, and I opened the window by the head of my bed. It was starting to snow. Soft, cool flakes drifted in out of the darkness over my face and hair.

Morning came. Still there was no change in the pains. The nurse was getting restive.

"I shall have to leave you and see to the rest of my patients," she said.

"How long will you be?" I asked rather apprehensively. "I don't think I shall get much warning at the end."

"About two hours," she said.

It was very quiet in the house after she had gone. Victoria had got the weenybedes up and given them breakfast, while Steven cooked breakfast for the rest of them. I didn't want to eat anything. Victoria was doing the washing when Steven came up to see me.

"Can you do the grocery order?" he asked. "We ought to take it today."

"Of course—it's Saturday." It seemed ages since Friday.

I sat up and tried to think about groceries.

"A pound of margarine, a pound of bacon, a dozen eggs—wait a minute..."

A pain caught me in the middle of it, and I lay back and waited until it was past.

"A packet of cornflakes, four pounds of sugar, seven pounds of potatoes—do we need paraffin?"

"No, not yet. I can cycle with these things, can't I, then Geoffrey can stay with you, and I'll get back quicker."

"Three pounds of flour, half a pound of cooking fat, baby foods..."—then another pain.

At last it was finished. "Be as quick as you can!" I said.

After he had gone the pains started coming quicker and stronger. The nurse had left her gas and air apparatus by the side of my bed, but it was turned off. I had always thought the effect was more mental than physical—now I held the mask to my face, and breathed into it with each pain. I looked at my watch. The nurse had been gone an hour.

Steven came back. The pains were coming increasingly stronger. It became impossible to pretend that the gas and air mask was deadening them any longer.

The nurse had been gone an hour and a half. And the baby was going to be born very soon now.

"Geoffrey," I called. He was waiting outside my door. "Tell Steven to run down to the telephone and ring the doctor, and the nurse's house. Tell them the baby is coming now—its head is down—and get someone to come *quickly*."

Steven set off down the field as fast as he could, while Geoffrey stood by the window watching. "He's gone through the field gate!" he told me a few minutes later. He continued to watch anxiously.

The pains were getting rapidly worse, and the intervals in between seemed awfully short.

"Is anyone coming yet?" I called to Geoffrey for about the tenth time.

Suddenly he called excitedly, "I can see Steven coming in the gate!—and the nurse is with him!—*and* the doctor!" His voice shook. Another pain got hold of me.

"How near are they now?"

"They're halfway up the field—the doctor's running—he's nearly at the top—the nurse has slipped on the mud—she's coming up behind now—they're at our gate—they're coming up the path—they're at the door…!" he broke off and ran down the stairs to meet them.

A minute later doctor and nurse were in the room, taking off their outdoor things and putting on overalls, masks, gloves—"If only they'd just get *on* with it," I thought.

"Well, how long is it going to be now?" asked the doctor.

"About two minutes," I said faintly.

The nurse turned on the gas and air, handed me the mask, and told me to turn on my side—much to my annoyance, as I wanted to be delivered on my back, because it's so much nicer to be able to *see* the baby born—but I was in no condition to argue.

I took the mask and pushed. I didn't know that the head was out, until I heard the baby cry—then the doctor said, "It's a girl!"

I twisted round to look. She had a lot of dark hair, a turned-up nose, and the funniest little face I'd ever seen. I lay back, feeling rather shaky, while the doctor and nurse did all the seemingly endless things that have to be done after a baby is born. But at last it was over, and the doctor left, telling the four excited children that all was well. The nurse put the baby, wrapped in a blanket, into my arms.

Victoria tiptoed into the room, and stood looking down at her. She didn't speak, and I heard her catch her breath.

"Has she been bathed yet?" she whispered at last.

"No—you can see the nurse bath her in a minute."

"I heard her first cry," Victoria whispered. "I was feeding Nicholas in the weenybedes' room, and I left the door open…"

Geoffrey came in with a cup of tea for me. "Steven and Helen are getting lunch," he said. "Oh—isn't she sweet!"

He stood gazing at her.

"Do you want anything to eat? How much does she weigh?"

"Seven pounds. I'm awfully hungry," I told him. "I haven't had anything since yesterday breakfast!"

"I'll tell Steven to bring you something up," he said.

Victoria stayed to see the baby bathed. Then the nurse laid her in her cradle, and put the cradle on the other side of my bed.

"I'll leave her there so you can pick her up yourself," she said. Getting on her hat and coat, she paused. "It's two o'clock now—can you manage yourself this evening?"

"Oh, yes," I said. "Will she need a feed today?"

"No—just change her and keep her clean—I'll come in tomorrow morning."

She left, and Steven brought me in a plate of scrambled egg.

"It was a good thing you got the doctor and nurse so quickly," I told him.

"I couldn't speak to the nurse, she was out still," he explained,

Victoria with the sheep.

Victoria with Moonlight.

Steven wheeling Nicholas and
Christopher in the barrow.

Christopher's and Nicholas's
birthday tea.

Christopher goes exploring.

Helen on the pond

"but the doctor said he'd come straight away, and both he and the nurse arrived at the bottom of the drift as I came back from the phone." He looked indignant. "The nurse *would* stop to wipe the mud off her feet at the door," he complained. "I told her the baby's head was right down, you wouldn't worry about the mud!"

"Well—we managed it, despite the *mud*!" I said.

Helen, Geoffrey and Victoria came in, and the four of them gazed wonderingly at the tiny scrap of life now sleeping peacefully in the cradle.

"Isn't she lovely?" said Helen.

"Look at her tiny hands!" said Steven.

"She's all ours now, isn't she?" said Geoffrey proudly.

"Can I help you change her?" asked Victoria.

"I shall want you to help," I told her. "I've never handled one as young as this before!"

I lay back, conscious of a deep contentment. At last I had my baby all to myself from the first hour. This is as it should be, I thought. It was worth all the worrying and arguing about the field. Suddenly it seemed that I had nothing in the world to worry about any more. The job I had been doing for the last nine months was completed. I needed to do nothing now but rest.

"What shall we call her?" Victoria asked.

The snow was still falling softly outside.

"Carol," I said.

11

The Coming of Spring

It was snowing when Carol was born, and although I didn't notice it until the next day, when I was allowed to get out of bed, the ground was already white with snow.

The next morning I heard a steady "drip—drip" coming from the roof over my head, and saw a damp patch spreading over the ceiling. Geoffrey volunteered to get a ladder and investigate. He found a tile dislodged on the roof, and climbed up to replace it, while I lay in bed and listened in some trepidation to the sounds of his movements above.

By the third day, when I got up and came downstairs for tea, the snow had gone; and by the end of the week, when I was up and about again, it was warm, and the sun was shining, and there was spring in the air. I went out and walked round the garden, looking at the green shoots of the bulbs Steven and I had planted, coming up in the flower beds and in the grass.

Victoria and I took Nicholas and Christopher for a walk, Geoffrey carrying the push-chair down the field and back, and we watched new-born lambs playing in the fields up the road.

One morning when Victoria and I were doing the washing, Carol suddenly started to cry. At the same moment Steven came running down the stairs.

"No wonder Carol's crying!" he said. "There's a great big Field-Marshal making a terrific noise right under her window!"

"Up here?" I asked incredulously.

"Yes—they've come to do something to the field!" he explained, disappearing out of the back door.

I went upstairs to comfort Carol. Looking out of the window, I saw what he meant. A large Field-Marshal tractor was standing outside, its engine roaring. I picked Carol up and comforted her until the tractor had moved away.

"They're drilling barley on top of the wheat," Geoffrey told us later. "Most of the wheat was spoiled by the wet."

Anyway, at last they harrowed the field, and ran the Field-Marshal up and down our track; and we began to think spring had come.

Victoria and I bathed the weenybedes together again, and after two weeks, when the nurse stopped coming, we bathed Carol together too. Like all babies, Carol was the most adorable baby that ever was. She wasn't pretty, but she had blue eyes with dark lashes, and brown hair, slightly curling, with gold lights in it, which was almost fair at the roots. As it grew the new hair was all golden, although the ends were still brown, so Helen said she was really piebald. She smiled very early, the sweetest smile we had ever seen, and when not disturbed by Field-Marshals, she hardly ever cried.

Christopher and Nicholas loved her, and Christopher ran to kiss her whenever he came into my room. I had never had a baby sleeping in my room before—the others had all had rooms of their own. I didn't know before how comforting it was to hear the small breathing close to me all night, and be awakened in the morning by the sweetness of her bubbling conversation, and see her tiny hands making little grabs at the air over the edge of her cradle.

One morning when Carol was a month old, the weather changed. It grew very cold, with a bitter north-east wind, and began to snow; and all our cats and kittens curled up in a pile three deep in front of the sitting-room fire.

In the evening it was still snowing, and the babies' washing on the line was as wet as when we hung it out. I left it there, hoping the weather would improve by the next day. But it snowed all night, and froze hard. In the morning we found we were snowed in, and Geoffrey had to dig a path to the gate. Our washing was no longer visible as clothes and nappies, but looked like lumps of frozen snow at intervals along the snow-covered line.

We needed various supplies, and Geoffrey volunteered to walk into the village for them—cycling was out of the question. He set off into a north-east blizzard, dressed in breeches, an old thick sweater of mine over his own pullover, and my old burberry, with a wool scarf tied over his head. He looked as if he was crossing the Antarctic.

Steven went on digging paths to the sheds, and Victoria and I tackled the problem of the washing. While we started on the day's wash, Helen went out to get the previous day's in.

After a few minutes she came back. "I can't get the pegs off!" she complained. "Can I have the pincers?"

Everything was frozen solid. It took her over half an hour to get it all off the line, using the pincers to undo each peg. She carried it back into the house in solid lumps. We put the whole lot into the bath, filled with warm water; thawed it out, put it through the wringer, and hung it all up again in the sitting-room. By then Helen and Steven had had enough of the snow, and curled up by the fire with the cats to thaw their fingers, while Victoria fed Christopher and Nicholas, and I got into bed to feed Carol, holding her under the bedclothes to keep us both warm.

It was ten o'clock in the morning when Geoffrey left; he got back at three o'clock in the afternoon. He was so covered with frozen snow that we had to thaw him out in the kitchen before he could get his clothes off.

"There were snowdrifts above my head blocking all the roads," he told us. "I had to leave the roads and go over fields. There are two buses abandoned on the main road, and a lorry overturned in the ditch. When I got to the shop they said I was the only person from outside the village who had got through today. There won't be any bread tomorrow if it's still like this, they won't be able to get through. And there won't be any milk today—the van had to turn back at the church. I should think we could get some from the farm at the bottom of the drift, though. Shall I go and see?"

"I think you've done enough," I said. "You need a meal next."

"I'll go," said Steven, and set off wrapped up in more thick woollies of mine, taking all the jugs we had available. He came back with two full ones.

"I'll have to go down again for the rest, I couldn't carry any more. They can let us have all the milk we want—the milk lorry couldn't get through either, and they've got twenty gallons of milk they can't get rid of!"

All that night it went on freezing and snowing. The next day the snow had stopped, but it was still freezing hard.

"I'll have to walk into the village and get the bread," Geoffrey said.

"You'd better get some tinned meat and things too," I told him. "Whatever they've got—we shan't get anything else until the roads are clear."

It was late afternoon again when he got back. "The roads are worse," he reported. "It's been drifting, and the drifts are well over six feet high. I got the bread, but they hadn't a tin of meat or anything left. Everyone in the village has been buying up food supplies, and there won't be anything more coming in until the roads are clear again."

"What do we do, then?" demanded Helen.

"Perhaps I could walk in to the town, if I started early and went over the fields," suggested Geoffrey, as he warmed up over the fire with hot soup and coffee. "We'll see what it's like in the morning."

It snowed again in the night, and went on freezing. Next morning Geoffrey set out again, and walked the five miles to the town. He came back, laden with supplies, just before dark.

"We're standing up to the weather better than they are in the town," he told us. "Half the houses have got tiles off there. The roads are completely blocked, but it wasn't too bad going over the fields. I should think there'll be a flood when it thaws!"

That night it didn't quite freeze, and the wind went down. The next morning it started to thaw; and Steven reported that we were nearly out of paraffin. As the house was entirely heated by paraffin, this was serious.

"Can we get through with the barrow?" asked Steven. "It's no good fetching one gallon—we use that in a day. It'll have to be the five-gallon can."

"We'd better start off with the barrow and see how far we can get," said Geoffrey. "What we need is a Sno-Cat!"

After they had left, the thaw became more rapid. Sliding, falling snow kept flopping down outside the windows and dropping off the trees. Geoffrey and Steven got back soaked, but they had got through.

"The water-splash is up the road ten yards each side," Geoffrey said. "It was too deep to wade through, but we got past along the bank."

"The barrow overturned twice," said Steven, "but we got it up again, and we didn't lose any paraffin."

"We had to drag it through the snow that's still lying," said Geoffrey. "It's horrible now, all brown slush."

"They were surprised to see us with the barrow at the shop," Steven said. "And we've brought the post—it's only just come through, there hasn't been any in for the last three days."

"Anyway, it looks as if it's over now," said Geoffrey cheerfully. "It's funny—Carol will never remember anything about this!"

Upstairs in my bedroom, where the stove had been kept burning night and day, Carol lay in her cradle peacefully asleep.

The next day the bread was delivered, and so was the milk, although the milk van got trapped between the flooded water-splash and a fresh flood that poured off the fields on the other side of the village, and had to be towed out by tractor. Gradually the flood water went down, and within a few weeks faint green spikes of corn began to appear all over our field; and our daffodils were in flower. Winter was over.

With the coming of spring, the weenybedes began to emerge again, like little hibernating animals, to a fresh burst of activity. Christopher was now two, and starting to talk; Nicholas was one, and getting on to his feet. Nicholas was sturdy and broad, and what he lacked in balance he made up for in determination. He would set off at a run, his arms waving wildly in all directions in the effort to keep upright—and then plonk!—he would sit down abruptly, with a look of great surprise, and in a minute or two would be up and staggering round again. Christopher was not at first very pleased about this, apparently thinking that he was the walking weenybede, and Nicholas the crawling one, and every time he saw Nicholas on his feet he would rush up and gently push him down again, consoling Nicholas's angry protests with a kiss—but after a time he got used to it. They began to really play together, sharing toys more or less amicably, and having occasional battles, when they rolled over and over on the floor like puppies, bashing each other furiously without either appearing to mind.

Christopher was developing a mechanical bent, and it was his great delight to get hold of the pincers or pliers and find something to mend. This usually resulted in its falling to pieces, but the idea was the same.

He liked paddling in the stream at the bottom of the drift, and when at last it dried up he was most indignant, and stood peering into the bank, trying to find it.

"Gone!" he cried desolately, "Gone!"

At the first sign of a shower he would rush into the house and fetch the washing bowls, crying "Naining, naining!" and insist that we should get the washing in.

Nicholas was a problem in wet weather, for we could not keep shoes on him, and as soon as he saw the door open he was out of it and halfway across the garden. His feet were so broad that I couldn't get boots to fit him—even Christopher's wouldn't go on—and when I did manage to get a pair of sandals that he could wear, he carefully took them off and threw them away.

Our playpen was by now too broken for its original use, but instead we folded it and put it across the doorway of the nursery to make a playroom, wedged in place by the end of our dining-table, and there Christopher and Nicholas played after they had had their breakfast, while we had ours. This worked very well until Christopher discovered that he could throw things. Breakfast then became a hazardous meal, when small hard objects were apt to fly across the table without warning, taking a coffee cup or a jug of milk with them on the way.

After breakfast Nicholas stayed in the playroom, or went out in his push-chair, while Christopher ran round trying to help everyone, and removing the household tools and kitchen implements as fast as I put them away in the drawers. His favourite job was taking the empty milk bottles down to the safe by the road. We had given him a small wheelbarrow for Christmas, and he carefully stacked three bottles in this, and followed Steven or Helen, with the rest of the bottles in the big barrow, down the field.

One morning I had just come downstairs, in my dressing-gown, to make early tea before giving Carol her feed, when I heard Steven shouting from the landing, "The cattle are out! They're all over the front field!"

Steven, Geoffrey and I ran out. The gate to the drift at the bottom of the field was open—and our garden gate had been broken off its hinges during the blizzard, so our garden was exposed.

Geoffrey and Steven, who were dressed, ran down the field to head the cattle off from the road. I stood in our gateway, shoo-ing them away from our garden as they came past. Round the back of the house, too, there was a gap in the fence, where the wire had been broken. Hastily pulling on boots, I ran round the house, and stood in that gap, while Geoffrey and Steven drove the cows back into their field. The wind was cold, and I was wearing a nightdress designed for feeding babies, not chasing cows.

"You'd better mend that fence today, and that gate," I told Geoffrey and Steven when they came in. "Where did they get out?"

"Through the barn," said Geoffrey, "but I've stopped it up with a hurdle now."

Later in the morning, Victoria came running in from the garden in great excitement.

"They're putting four horses and a little foal on the big field!"

I looked out of the window. A cattle float stood in the drift, and two men were driving the horses up the track—a grey cob, a black pony, a white pony, a black mare, and an exquisite black and white piebald foal.

When the men had gone, Victoria took Nicholas and Christopher out to look at them. I joined her, carrying Carol in my arms. We stood at the gate, and Victoria held out a lump of sugar in the palm of her hand.

The mare put her head over the gate and took the sugar. The foal came up behind her, and sniffed at Christopher. I held Carol up to see them, and the mare blew gently at her. Carol laughed, put out her hand, and stroked the mare's nose.

That afternoon Geoffrey was out repairing the gate when we heard the sound of an engine outside.

Christopher cried, "Car, car!" and ran out to see. It was our landlord, unloading a large crate.

A few minutes later we heard the car drive away, and Geoffrey went past the window, carrying in his arms a large white goose.

"I've got to put it on the pond!" he called to us.

We all ran out to watch, Victoria carrying Nicholas. Geoffrey put the goose down at the edge of the pond, and it floated gracefully away to the other side.

Christopher watched in delight, and Nicholas reached out his hands to it.

"Isn't it beautiful?" said Helen.

"We must give it some bread," said Geoffrey, "so it will stay here."

"Can we feed it now?" asked Steven. We all watched as he threw the bread into the pond, and the goose swung round and dived for the pieces.

"We've got another neighbour!" said Helen.

"I hope it doesn't like daffodils!" I said. "It can easily fly over our fence."

"I hope it won't frighten the baby moorhens," said Victoria.

"He's bringing a gander later. Perhaps they'll bring up young," Geoffrey said.

The goose rose up in the water and flapped its wings, gleaming like snow in the spring sunlight.

12

Hawthorn, Hares and Rabbits

"It's hares and rabbits night," said Victoria, as we sat at supper.

"And tomorrow is the first of May," I said. "If you go out early in the morning on the first of May and wash your face in the dew off a hawthorn bush, they say it will make you beautiful for ever."

"Can we do it?" asked Victoria and Helen together.

"I don't see why not," I said, "if tomorrow is a dewy sort of day."

"Will you come too?" asked Helen.

I looked at my reflection in the mirror over the mantelpiece, and put back a strand of hair that had got loose and was tickling my nose.

"I think I'd better," I said.

"Couldn't we take Carol?" Victoria asked suddenly. "It would be a sort of christening present—like the fairy stories."

"Well—she's rather little to go out at dawn, but I don't suppose it would hurt her," I said. "If it's a fine morning—and anyway, there won't be any dew on the bushes if it's not."

"Don't forget hares and rabbits, tonight," said Steven. "It should be a special hares and rabbits night before the first of May."

So when I went round tucking in that night I said "Goodnight— *hares!*" over each bed, and waited until I got a sleepy response before going quickly out, so as not to give rise to any further conversation, and shutting the doors.

Christopher and Nicholas being too little to understand saying "Hares", I said it for them; and lastly murmured "Hares" to Carol as she lay in my arms after finishing her feed, before I tucked her into her cradle and we both went to sleep.

I awoke early in the morning and after a few minutes of blankness remembered, and said "Rabbits!" to Carol, and then went round the children's beds saying "Rabbits!" until I got "Rabbits" in response.

Victoria sat up and pushed the hair out of her eyes.

"Rabbits!—it's the first of May," she said. "Shall we get up now?"

"Yes, get dressed and come down as soon as you're ready," I said. "I'll dress Carol and feed her, and then we'll go."

Half an hour later the four of us left the house and walked up the back loke, with Carol wrapped up in a shawl in my arms. It was certainly a dewy morning; the grass was heavy with it, each blade shining with silver and diamonds—"Much nicer than the things in jewellers' windows," Victoria said.

We reached a quiet field halfway up the loke, and, Victoria holding Carol while I climbed, we got over the gate. On the other side of the field was a hawthorn bush, spangled with shining dew.

Helen and Victoria and I shook the glittering drops onto our hands, and bathed our faces. Then I carefully took a few drops on one fingertip and gently stroked Carol's face with it. She opened her eyes wide in surprise, and then smiled.

"She likes it much better than warm water and cotton wool!" said Victoria.

Together we stood in a semi-circle, facing the sun, and letting the growing warmth of it dry our faces. Behind us stood four black-and-white cows, who had come up quietly while we were dew-bathing, watching us with placid interest.

"Oh, look!" said Helen, turning round, "they've been washing their faces in the dew too!"

"Well, they're certainly very beautiful cows," I said.

We walked slowly back over the field, followed at a little distance by the cows.

Suddenly Victoria bent down and cried out, "Look!"

Helen and I turned and saw her holding a small brown furry thing in her hands.

"Look—it's a baby rabbit—isn't it?" she said in a puzzled voice.

Long ears, big dark eyes, and fur so soft it was like a baby bird's down. I stroked it gently with one fingertip.

"No," I said, "I think it's a leveret—a baby hare. You must put it back where you found it, or the mother hare may not be able to find it when she comes."

Gently Victoria laid the leveret back in its nest in the long grass.

As we walked back she said, "I've never seen a leveret before. It must have been because of hares and rabbits night. I *wish* I had a hare or a rabbit of my own."

"So do I," said Helen.

Perhaps there was something in hares and rabbits night after all, because Steven came in at dinner time full of excitement.

"I met our landlord up the road," he told us, "and he said would we like a pair of rabbits—he's got a litter ready to sell."

"Oh—could we?" cried Victoria.

"Did you see them?" asked Helen.

"What kind are they, and how much?" I asked.

"Yes, he showed them to me," said Steven. "They're black-and-white ones,—I think they're Old English—they're quite small, and he wants two shillings each."

"We'd have to build a hutch for them first," said Geoffrey.

"What could we make it out of?" asked Steven.

"Well—there's that old wardrobe in the shed," I said. "You can have that—and I think there's some old wire-netting in the wood-pile. You should be able to do something with that."

"Let's go and have a look at it," said Geoffrey.

"If you can make a hutch, you can have them," I said.

The next few days were filled with the sounds of sawing and hammering, interspersed with various exclamations as one or other of the boys hammered a thumb instead of a nail; but it was done at last, and a most impressive-looking rabbit hutch stood on an old kitchen table—which I hadn't really finished with, begged from me by Steven—under an apple tree.

Geoffrey, Steven, Victoria and Helen took a basket and went to collect the rabbits.

It was getting dark when they came back, and they brought the basket into the sitting-room, and put it down on the floor. Steven lifted the lid, and inside were two small, soft, adorable black-and-white rabbits.

"Aren't they lovely?" said Victoria.

"Get them straight into the hutch, and let them settle down," I said. "They're bound to be scared after being carried so far."

"We have to feed them on crushed oats, and bread baked in the oven, and hogweed," said Steven. "Can I bake them some bread now?"

"No—wait till I have the oven on in the morning," I said. "Give them some green-stuff now, if it's light enough to see to pick it."

"I know where there's some hogweed!" cried Helen, and ran out.

"Where do you get crushed oats?" I inquired.

"From the baker, I should think," said Geoffrey. "They sell meal and corn, don't they?"

So the two rabbits were moved into the old wardrobe, and Geoffrey covered them up for the night with an old burberry of mine which I still wore occasionally, but not enough to be able to refuse when he asked if he could take it; and I went to bed conscious of having added the responsibility of two more living creatures to my family.

My first thought when I woke the next morning was again "Rabbits!" but these were real rabbits, and I hastily got out of bed and looked out of the window to see if they were all right. Geoffrey was already there, taking off the cover, and the rabbits were hopping cautiously towards the wire-netting front looking for something to eat. I sighed with relief, and went down to make early tea.

They settled down happily enough, the only drawback being the amount of time we all spent watching them; including myself—and the cats.

After the first few days, most of the cats lost interest; but Big Huge was fascinated by them and spent hours curled up on top of the hutch, or underneath it, watching the two rabbits hopping about inside. But they appeared quite unaware of his presence, and he never made any attempt to break in.

And then one morning I heard a cry from Steven, and ran out, followed by Geoffrey, to see Big Huge running away from the hutch as if pursued by the devil, while Steven was standing there in tears. And the little buck rabbit was lying on its side close to the wire-netting, with blood pouring out of a tiny wound over its heart.

"Big Huge was just sitting there—looking at them," sobbed Steven, "and suddenly he hit out—just once—through the wire—and the blood started pouring out—and then he ran away… Is it dying? Is it going to die…?"

Geoffrey and I looked closely at the rabbit, lying with closed eyes, while its life-blood poured away.

"I'm afraid so, Steven," I said. "It must have been an extraordinary stroke—he hasn't injured it at all, except for that one wound—one claw must have gone straight into the heart. He might have missed altogether—he couldn't have known what he was going to do. It isn't in any pain—it must have become unconscious at once—and it's dying fast. Lift it out, Geoffrey, and put it in a basket in the shed—and clear out all the straw with blood on it—it will upset the little doe, and she's frightened enough already."

Steven put his hands over his face and turned away. Victoria and Helen stood watching, tears running down their faces.

"Big Huge knows he's done wrong," said Helen tearfully. The cat was sitting by the gate now, looking apprehensively over his shoulder at the rabbit hutch.

"I don't think he meant to kill it," I said. "Cats don't kill rabbits like that in the ordinary way—they bite into the neck. I think he must have made a dab at it just to see what happened—and now he looks quite shocked."

"I don't think he's ever been sure that they were rabbits, really," said Geoffrey. "He's still not sure, and he's done something he doesn't understand."

"Perhaps he'll keep away from the hutch in future," said Victoria.

We gently lifted out the dying rabbit, and Geoffrey cleared out all the stained straw from the hutch. The little doe sat mournfully at the back of the hutch, but she came forward and nibbled a leaf of hogweed when Steven offered it to her.

"She'll be all right, when she gets over the fright," I said.

"Shall I cover her up for a bit?" suggested Geoffrey. "She'll feel safer in the dark."

So we put the cover over the hutch, and went sadly back to the house, where Christopher and Nicholas, shut in their playroom, were clamouring to get out.

The cottages up the 'loke'—

Victoria with Christopher and Nicholas

Nicholas and Victoria with Snowy

"Can we get another rabbit?" Steven asked.

"Yes; she must have a mate," I said. "You and Geoffrey can go and see if our landlord has another one, this evening."

But they came back disappointed. "He's sold all the young rabbits now," Geoffrey said. "We'll have to find someone else who has one for sale."

The next morning I went out early to catch a train into the town. Coming round the corner of the house on my way up the back loke, I saw Big Huge sitting by the shed.

"Ahhhh! You old devil!" I said crossly.

And then looking up, I saw our landlord standing a few yards away, where he could not see Big Huge, with a completely astonished expression on his face.

I said "Good morning!" and he replied "Good morning!" in a still more puzzled way.

It was not until I was halfway up the loke that I realized that, not seeing the cat, he must have thought that my previous remark was addressed to him...

Whether Big Huge took my rebuke to heart, or whether he was really frightened by what he had done, or just lost interest in the rabbits anyway, he made no further attempts to touch the remaining occupant of the hutch, and no longer sat watching her—in fact he behaved as if hutch, apple tree and rabbits had ceased to exist.

Time went on, and we continued to make inquiries about getting another rabbit, but no one had any for sale. Our little doe grew steadily, became very tame, and appeared perfectly happy; and we called her Anna, because as Steven said, she was a very merry widow.

13

Growing Up

With young children nothing ever stands still. As fast as you establish a routine, someone grows out of it, and you have to introduce a new one. After Carol was born I felt that I needed to let one or two extra hours into each day, like a piece of material into a dress which was rapidly growing too small.

A good deal of extra time was taken up in feeding Carol. I gave up timing her feeds and let her suck as long as she wanted to. Often over her last feed we both fell asleep, and I would awake in the small hours of the morning to find her still clinging to me with a little rosebud mouth, very warm and pink in my arms, smiling adorably when I looked down at her face. But somehow we managed to rearrange everything else round her, and everything fitted in.

As time went on, all three weenybedes grew almost visibly day by day, and Nicholas started to talk; and the first word he learned to say was "No." He said it in a variety of tones of voice and somehow managed to make it convey an incredible number of shades of meaning. I played a game with him, consisting of my saying, "Shall I tell you something, Nicky?" to which he would reply with a sweet smile, "No!" And I would say, "*No?*" and he would say, "*No*"—and this went on until he gave up and let me whisper "Sweet Nicky!" in his ear, and he rolled over shouting with laughter.

One afternoon Geoffrey and Steven were out in the village, and Helen and Victoria had taken Christopher to look at the horses. I was alone in the house with Carol, and Nicholas was sitting in his push-chair by the rabbit hutch, watching Anna, which often kept him happily occupied for hours. I was waiting for the milk to come for the weenybedes' tea, and when I heard the milk van coming down the road I ran down the field to fetch it, telling Nicholas I wouldn't be long. As I started to come up the field again with the milk, I heard him start to cry.

I couldn't see what was wrong, but knowing he might have rocked his push-chair over and fallen out backwards—which he did quite regularly, usually taking advantage of it to crawl out and run round the garden—I wanted to reassure him as soon as possible, and couldn't get up the field with the milk in time. So I shouted at the top of my voice, "Shall I tell you something, Nicky?"—and there was a pause in the crying and then, in a loud, determined voice, Nicholas shouted back, "No!"

I arrived to find him sitting on the ground beside his chair, unhurt and laughing, and I took him indoors and put him in the high-chair while I prepared his tea.

Both Christopher and Nicholas loved biscuits and were constantly raiding the biscuit tin if it was accidentally left within their reach—and that included any table onto which, with the help of a chair, they could climb. Unfortunately, Nicholas's idea of eating biscuits was to take one bite out of each biscuit and then throw it away while he went on to the next. Quite often, if the two of them were left alone in the sitting-room for a few minutes, we would come back to find Nicholas sitting cross-legged on the table, surrounded by biscuits each with one bite taken out of them, and Christopher standing on the table beside him, feeding him with those he hadn't started on yet.

They both loved the cats, and when we had two new kittens Nicholas practically adopted them and settled down with them on the hearthrug, where they seemed to think he was just a large-size kitten himself. They must have been very well-nourished kittens, for they had all the leavings of baby foods that the weenybedes didn't want; and Christopher soon realized this, and when he had eaten all he wanted would push his plate away, saying, "No, tittens—give tittens."

As they grew older, Christopher and Nicholas developed widely differing temperaments. At bedtime, before settling down in his cot, Christopher asked every night, "Book, book," and lay down contentedly "reading" until he fell asleep. The only drawback was that, like Geoffrey at the same age, he demanded a *fresh* book every night. Nicholas was no sooner put in his cot than he was on his feet again, holding on to the top rail and bouncing with all the energy that he didn't seem to have expended in running about nearly all day. Regularly his cot broke under this treatment, and Nicholas had to be rescued and nursed on my lap while Geoffrey or Steven mended the cot. One night, after a lot of bouncing, there was silence, and I thought he must have gone to sleep for once without causing his cot to disintegrate first. But when I went up to tuck him in, I found the bottom of the cot had fallen through, as usual, and the side had fallen in—and Nicholas was lying curled up in the wreckage, unhurt and fast asleep. There was only one way to persuade Nicholas to settle at night. When I put him in his cot I gave him a pink woolly bed jacket of mine. This he grabbed with a happy smile, wrapped it all round himself, and settled down looking like a pink woolly cocoon.

One morning I said to Victoria, "We ought to cut the wee-nybedes' hair."

Christopher had a bunch of soft curls falling into his eyes, and Nicholas had a thick cushion of curls all over his head, and both of them got it pulled when we tied their feeders behind their necks at meals.

So we put them one after the other in the high chair, and I took a pair of scissors and started clipping. I am no good at hairdressing, and even a trained barber might find difficulty in cutting hair which didn't stay in the same place for two consecutive seconds. But we got it done at last, and the other children all wanted to have curls to keep from the pathetic-looking little heaps of brown and gold hair all over the floor. Considering all things, they didn't look too bad when I'd finished; and the only casualty was a blister on my finger where the scissors had pressed into it while I was cutting through Nicholas's thick cushion of hair.

"Now people won't keep saying they're girls!" said Victoria.

Soon after this, notices began to appear on trees and gate-posts announcing garden fêtes in all the surrounding villages; and when ours grew near, the children wanted to go.

"We can't take *all* the babies," I said.

"We could take Christopher and Nicholas, though," said Victoria. We had a second push-chair now. "And Carol would be all right at home for a little while—one of us could come back early to be with her."

So we arranged it. On the afternoon of the fête, Victoria and Geoffrey set off first, walking and pushing Christopher and Nicholas. Steven and Helen got ready while I fed Carol and dressed myself, and then we followed on our bicycles, leaving Carol safely in her cradle.

When we arrived at the vicarage garden we found Victoria and Geoffrey with the weenybedes at the hoop-la stall.

"I've won you a cake of soap!" Geoffrey informed me.

"I've been trying to get that toy horse for Christopher," said Victoria.

"I'll have a try," said Steven.

We got a supply of rings and Steven started to throw. One ring hit the stall and bounced back. Christopher, who had been watching from behind Victoria's skirt, came forward and picked it up.

"Oh, let him try!" cried Helen.

So we gave Christopher a new ring and waited to see what he would do. He stood firmly in front of the stall and hurled the ring towards it, but it fell short. Then he held out his hand for another. His next ring skimmed over the stall and landed at the feet of the lady in charge. The next one he threw straight at her, hitting her in the chest. Everyone laughed, including the lady herself. Nicholas stood up in his chair and bounced up and down. Christopher was delighted and wanted more rings.

"I don't think he's got the right idea," I murmured to Geoffrey. "He thinks you have to ring the attendant!"

By this time a small crowd had gathered, and when Christopher landed a ring on the stall, everyone was pleased. He very nearly ringed the toy horse, and the lady gave it to him—perhaps to encourage him to aim in the right direction. When we finally left the hoop-la stall, Steven had won a jar of blackcurrant jam, Helen had won a bar of chocolate, and Christopher had nearly won a small girl, who had strayed behind the stall by mistake.

Victoria and I took Christopher and Nicholas and went to look at the other stalls, while Steven and Helen had a ride on the swings, and Geoffrey had a go at the coconut shy. When he joined us again, we had bought a tea cloth and a pink woolly jacket for Carol, and he had knocked down a coconut.

We collected Steven and Helen and made our way to the tea tent, where we sat down to ham sandwiches and strawberries and cream. Christopher sat next to Victoria, and I took Nicholas on my lap. I was looking round the tent when I heard a loud humming noise, like an outsize bumble bee. "Mmmmmmm!"—everyone looked round to see what it was. Then I realized—it was Nicholas, looking angelic—Steven had given him a spoonful of cream!

Before we finished tea the weenybedes began to grow restless, and Nicholas started bouncing on my lap. I should have moved my chair back from the table, but I didn't see the danger until it was too late. Suddenly Nicholas's hand caught my tea cup, and the whole of the contents poured over my dress.

There was nothing I could do but mop it up with my handkerchief—the dress was nylon, and would wash, anyway. We finished our tea and went out to dry it in the sun.

Victoria wanted to watch the children's dancing display, so Geoffrey took my bicycle and went home ahead of us to see that Carol was all right. Steven and Helen followed on their bicycles after the dancing was over, and Victoria and I walked back with the weenybedes.

When we got in, Geoffrey met us with Carol in his arms. "She's only just started to cry," he said, "and she stopped as soon as I picked her up."

As I started to go upstairs, Helen, having made a lightning change out of her best dress, ran through the sitting-room, pulling the door sharply behind her—and the handle fell off.

"Oh dear, it's broken," she said contritely, picking up the metal thumb rest that used to work the latch, off the floor.

"You *have* done it now!" said Steven. "Once the door is shut, no one in the sitting-room will be able to get out!"

"I know—I can mend it!" said Helen.

"How?" asked Geoffrey.

Helen ran into the kitchen and got a tea-spoon out of the drawer. "Can I have this?" she asked.

She put it through the hole under the latch where the handle had been. It fitted in securely, the bowl of the spoon taking the place of the thumb rest and the handle lifting the latch.

"Look—it works!"

"All right!" I said. "But we're probably the only house in the country with a tea-spoon for a door latch!"

Helen ran out to pick hogweed for Anna, and Victoria started getting the weenybedes' tea. I took Carol upstairs and changed her, now protesting loudly at all this delay in getting her milk.

When I laid her on my bed she watched every move I made with hopeful eyes, and her cries changed to shrieks of delight when I started to undress. Soon she was sucking contentedly in my arms.

Outside, Geoffrey and Steven were cutting the lawn, while Helen, with an armful of hogweed, sat and watched. The sound of their voices, and the scent of the new-mown grass, drifted in through my window.

Victoria brought Christopher and Nicholas into my room.

"Can they come in?" she asked. "They've had their tea."

They both climbed onto my bed and sat watching Carol. Christopher bent over her and kissed her, and Nicholas put his arms round my neck and kissed me. I lay back on the pillows, and Carol went on sucking contentedly.

"It's a sort of flower bed of weenybedes!" said Victoria.

14

The Merry Widow

One evening in July, Steven came back from the village laden with shopping and said he had met a man from the next village who had some rabbits for sale.

"They're half-grown ones, about Anna's age," he said. Anna was then five months old. "He can let us have a buck for seven-and-six—it wouldn't be any use getting a baby one now."

"All right," I said. "You'd better go up and get one."

"And soon we'll have baby rabbits," said Victoria delightedly.

"Yes—every six weeks, once they start," said Geoffrey. "And then the young rabbits will have young ones too..." and getting a pencil and paper, he started working out how many rabbits we should have at the end of a year...

"Stop!" I said. "We haven't got the first ones yet—and what we're going to do with the young ones when they do start breeding I don't know..."

"We can't *sell* them," said Victoria.

"We can have two each—that's fourteen," said Helen.

"I don't know if Carol would appreciate a rabbit just yet," I said. "Anyway, get the buck, Steven—and we'll see what happens..." Although privately I had visions of our being overrun with hundreds of black-and-white rabbits, which none of us would ever have the heart to sell, give away, or destroy.

That evening Steven and Helen went off on their bicycles with the basket and returned some time later with a half-grown and very frightened black-and-white buck rabbit. We put him in the hutch with Anna, gave him a good feed, and left them in peace.

He soon settled down and became as tame as Anna, and as he was to marry the merry widow, we called him Danilo. It soon became apparent that Anna intended to keep him in order; she chivvied him round the hutch, bit him, and snatched the choicest leaves of hogweed from him; and he responded with a devotion to her which was touching, although it appeared quite undeserved.

The weeks went by, the rabbits grew steadily, and nothing else happened. Christopher and Nicholas ran happily backwards and forwards to the hutch, feeding them with greenstuff and baked bread—particularly baked bread, for they were very fond of it themselves, and whenever we gave them a piece to take out to the hutch, they ate some of it on the way.

As the end of summer approached, we began to wonder whether we ought to leave the hutch out under the tree; and then one night a gale blew up, and I was awakened by the howling of the wind round the house, and I shivered, thinking of the rabbits. As soon as it was light I got up and went to the landing window—to see the hutch, blown right off the table, lying on its back on the grass.

I ran into the boys' room and shook them awake. "Geoffrey, Steven!" I called urgently. "Come quickly, the rabbits' hutch has blown over!"

Hastily pulling on coats and boots, we ran out. As we came near the hutch we heard sounds of movement; and when we looked in, we found both rabbits hopping about on what had been the back wall of their hutch, looking up at the suddenly changed view, rather startled but quite unharmed.

The boys righted the hutch and propped it up with sticks, and put in fresh straw. Later in the day, we moved it into the shed.

Time went on, and still we had two rabbits only, and no sign of any new arrivals. And then one morning Geoffrey came in from the shed and told us, "We're going to have baby rabbits at last. In about six weeks' time."

He was right. Six weeks later, Victoria came running in, bubbling over with excitement.

"Anna has got young!" she cried. "She's made a nest of her own fur under the straw in one corner of the hutch, and I can see the babies moving in it!"

"Oh, can I see?" cried Helen.

"Be careful," I said. "Rabbits don't like anyone to look at their young when they're first born."

But we all went out very quietly and looked in. No baby rabbits were visible, but there was the nest in a back corner of the hutch, and signs of movement were apparent under the straw and fur.

"Leave her alone now," I said as we went back to the house.

"Oughtn't we to take Danilo out?" asked Geoffrey. "He might destroy the young."

"He seems a friendly sort of buck so far," I said. "And I should think Anna will make him keep his distance, if necessary. Let's leave him for a bit and see—it would be nicer if they could bring up their family together."

Every day after that we cautiously looked in, and frequently Victoria or Helen would say that they had seen a baby rabbit's nose or ears or feet, showing through the pile of fur.

Then they began to report seeing whole baby rabbits; and at last Geoffrey said, "There are five—four black-and-white, and one pure black,"—and we were all able to watch them all running about the hutch.

It was obvious by now that Danilo had no intention of harming them; and as they grew, he showed, if anything, more affection towards them than Anna did. We frequently found her sitting at the front of the hutch quietly enjoying a lettuce or cabbage leaf, while Danilo lay at the back with the five babies nestling into his long fur. He was a contented, fatherly sort of rabbit, and one could quite easily imagine him settling down with a pipe and a newspaper for a nap in an armchair after Sunday dinner. I felt rather glad for his sake that *we* washed the rabbits' feeding dishes, as otherwise I could see Anna making him do the washing-up.

The first time that the rabbits had to be cleaned out after the young were born presented a problem. Two rabbits could be put in the basket we had fetched them in—but not seven.

Victoria and Helen came into the sitting-room one afternoon with their arms full of young rabbits.

"Please, could you look after them while we clean out the hutch?" they asked. "We won't be very long."

And they put five soft furry balls gently into my lap and went away. I sat there for half an hour, immobilized from all I ought to have been doing—baby-sitting for a family of rabbits.

When Victoria and Helen collected them again I said, "We'll have to make another hutch."

"Have you any more wardrobes?" inquired Geoffrey.

"*No*," I said. "Only the one I keep my clothes in—but I tell you what," I added with sudden inspiration, "there's that old linen basket in the bathroom. It's got a hinged lid at the top that would make a door if you put it on its side, and you could take out another side and put wire-netting over it..."

So the boys set to work, and soon the baby rabbits had a new hutch to move into when their bedding was being changed.

The next step was taking them outside. Geoffrey and Steven made a small pen of wire-netting, and we put all the rabbits into it on the grass. They hopped about, rather surprised, and Danilo tried to dig a hole in one corner—but only in a half-hearted sort of way, and he soon gave it up and just sat and nibbled the clover. The baby rabbits, pushed aside by Anna who was again expecting young, curled up comfortably round him.

Christopher and Nicholas were intrigued by the idea of the rabbits having a play-pen, and climbed in too. They fed Anna and Danilo with clover leaves, and the babies ran over their feet and sat on their legs.

"I wonder how many rabbits we'll have by next year," said Victoria. "We'll have to make a lot more hutches."

"Well, I haven't got any more wardrobes or linen baskets," I said firmly.

"Wouldn't it be better to build a bigger house for us," suggested Geoffrey, "and keep the rabbits in this one?"

"Anna and Danilo could have your bedroom, and the babies our rooms," Helen pointed out.

"And we could give them their meals in the kitchen," said Steven.

"It might even come to that," I sighed.

Five adorable bunches of black-and-white fluff hopped contentedly about in the sun.

15

Sugar in the Morning

Since the horses had been put on the big field, Victoria and Helen went out every evening to talk to them and feed them with sugar. One evening they came in breathless and disturbed.

"The white pony has got his back legs stuck in the wire fence," cried Victoria. "We've been trying to get him out, but we can't. Can you help?"

It was starting to get dark. I took a torch, and Geoffrey and I went out to look.

Between the big field, and the small field now golden with ripe wheat, there was a fence of pig-netting, put up between two willow trees. The white pony must have tried to get through into the wheat field, and caught his hind legs in the netting. He was standing there in the half light, the netting trampled down by his efforts to get free, firmly entangled about his legs and feet.

"I don't know how long he's been there," said Victoria. "The wire is all tangled about his hooves, dreadfully tightly, and it won't come out."

"I think we'd better get someone to come and see to him," I said.

"I'll go and telephone," said Geoffrey, and went off down the field.

It was quite dark when he got back.

"I couldn't get any reply," he said. "They must be out."

"What can we do?" cried Victoria. "We can't leave him there all night..."

"I could try to cut the wire away," said Geoffrey.

So we went out again, Geoffrey armed with a small pair of

pincers—the only suitable tool we had—and Victoria with lumps of sugar.

"Steady, Snowy, good boy," Victoria soothed the pony, and she fed him sugar and stroked his nose, while Geoffrey and I tackled the problem at the other end. I shone the torch on to the trampled wire, while Geoffrey knelt in the wet grass and examined the tangle of thick strands round the pony's hooves.

"However did he get it into this mess?" he exclaimed. "There's no end of it all twisted round his feet—lucky it's not barbed wire, though."

He started cutting through one of the strands. At first the pincers made no impression, and it seemed a long time before a Snap! told us the wire was cut through. After that another strand—and another...

The pony moved restlessly, and I watched apprehensively as Geoffrey's face bent closely over the iron-shod hoof. But Snowy seemed to understand what we were doing and made no attempt to kick. I stood holding the torch as still as I could, turning away every few minutes to shoo away the little black pony and the mare and foal, who kept coming up behind, curious to know what was going on, and blowing down the back of our necks.

"That should do it," Geoffrey said at last, and stood back. "Get him to lift his right foot, Victoria, and see if it's free."

Victoria moved to the pony's side and gently patted his leg.

"Up, boy, lift up," she said, and the pony raised his foot.

"No, it's still caught," I said. "Look, there's a bit of wire right under his shoe."

Geoffrey knelt down again and tugged at the wire, but it was stuck fast.

"I can't get it out," he said. "I'll have to cut it off at both sides."

Again he went to work with the pincers. The wire was stretched taut and difficult to get at, but at last it was through.

"Try again now, Victoria," he said.

Again Victoria persuaded the pony to lift his foot. This time the foot itself was free, but as he lifted it his leg caught against the top strand of the wire.

"I'll have to cut that too," said Geoffrey.

"You can't—it's much thicker than the rest," I said. "Can you get his foot up higher, Victoria?"

"He's frightened of falling, with the other foot still caught," said Victoria.

She pulled gently at the pony's leg. "Higher, Snowy, that's right," she urged him, while Geoffrey and I trod with all our strength on the wire.

The pony gave a final jerk of his leg, and got it over the wire and free.

"Steady, good boy," Victoria reassured him, and Geoffrey started work on the wire round the other leg.

Strand by strand the wire fell away, until again only the bottom strand was left.

"That's under the shoe too," said Geoffrey. "I'll have to cut it off—it's stuck right in like the other one. Get him to hold his foot up, Victoria."

Victoria came round to that side and gently raised the pony's foot. She knelt with the hoof in her hands, holding it steady while Geoffrey struggled with the wire.

As the final strand snapped through, Victoria stood up and patted the pony's side.

"It's all right now, Snowy!" she told him, and the pony sprang forward and cantered down the field into the darkness.

"We've done it!" said Geoffrey triumphantly.

Tired but elated, we went back to the house.

The next morning Geoffrey again telephoned our landlord, and told him what had happened and what we'd done.

"He says they'll have to get the wire out of his hooves and they may have to give him an anti-tetanus injection," he told us when he got back. "They're coming up with the vet."

Later in the morning we saw the car arrive, and Jean, our landlord's schoolgirl daughter, her mother, and the vet, walking past into the big field.

About half an hour later Jean came to the door.

"Please could anyone come to help?" she asked. "We can't catch Snowy, and if he doesn't have an anti-tetanus injection within two days he may die."

Geoffrey, Steven, and Victoria went out with her, and Helen and I followed with Christopher and Nicholas. But after a time the others came back. The vet, who was a stout man, was out of breath.

"I shouldn't think there's much wrong with his feet if he can run like that!" he said. "But you should get that wire out. Your daughter—" he turned to me—"got him to come right up to her, but he wouldn't let us get a halter on him."

"He's had a fright," I said, "and I expect he thinks he may be going to be trapped again. Could you leave the halter with us? He's used to us being here all the time, and perhaps Victoria could get it on him when he's calmed down a bit, and we could tie him up and let you know."

So the vet left, and Victoria came in with the halter, in a state of great excitement. In the afternoon she set off with a pocket full of lump sugar down the big field. But she came back downcast.

"He'll come up to me, but he's scared of being caught," she said. "As soon as I lift up my hand he swerves round and runs away. And I had to give half the sugar to the mare—she followed me all round the field. Have we got any more?"

"If not, I'll get some," I promised her. "I should wait until the morning. He's frightened now—first he had a fright last night, and then they chased him all over the place this morning—and all animals are scared of vets... they seem to be able to smell one a mile off. He may have got over it by tomorrow."

The next morning Victoria came downstairs early. As soon as breakfast was over, she went out, her pockets bulging with sugar. I was in the sitting-room with Christopher and Nicholas when she ran in, her eyes shining.

"He's in the barn. He followed me all the way up the field," she cried breathlessly. "Can you come and stop him getting out, while I get the halter?"

I ran out with Steven, climbed over the field gate and ran round to the entrance of the barn.

Snowy stood inside, watching the small gap in the wall on the other side, through which Victoria had gone.

We stood in the opening until Victoria came back, the halter in one hand and sugar in the other. She walked up to the pony, gave him a lump of sugar, and slipped the halter over his head. Snowy stood still, eyeing her affectionately.

"I didn't take the halter out with me at first," she explained, as she did up the straps round his face. "He's not used to seeing me with it, and the sight of it frightens him away. But he doesn't mind now..." and she patted his neck and kissed his nose.

"Shall I go and tell Jean?" asked Steven.

"No—I want to take him down to her myself!" said Victoria. "Can I?"

"Do you want me to go with you?" I asked.

"Yes, please!" said Victoria.

So leaving Steven and Helen in charge of the weenybedes, Victoria and I led Snowy down the field, up the road, through another drift, and down the lane leading to our landlord's house.

Snowy was still very nervous, and Victoria was very excited, and I wasn't sure when I said, "Steady now, steady!" whether I was talking to the girl or the horse.

But at last we reached the gates, and Victoria proudly led Snowy up the drive. She handed him over to Jean, and watched him led away to the stables.

As we walked back over the fields Victoria said wistfully, "I wish he was my horse! Jean doesn't really care for him—she leaves him on the field for weeks and weeks and never comes to see him, and I don't think she ever gives him sugar or anything—and he won't come to her, but he comes to me! I *wish* he was my horse..."

I looked down at her longing face, and sighed.

"We'll get you a pony. One day," I said.

We got back to the house in time to give the weenybedes a very late lunch. We had just finished our own lunch when there was a thudding of hooves outside, and we looked up to see Snowy trotting past our windows. Victoria and Steven ran out.

"They've put him back on the big field," Victoria said when she came in again. "They got the wire out of his hoof, and he didn't need an injection, it hadn't damaged the foot. And Jean says—" she caught her breath—"she doesn't want to keep him, she says he's snappy and greedy, and he gets too dirty in wet weather, because he's white—and she's going to get a new *brown* pony, and they're going to sell Snowy—" she broke off, flushed with indignation.

"He wouldn't get dirty if she groomed him properly. She'd get dirty if she never washed! And he *isn't* snappy or greedy, he only wants affection!—and when he's sold I'll never see him again…!"

She paused for breath, and two tears shone on her lashes.

"I suppose he'd cost an awful lot of money," said Steven.

"He's not a very young pony," said Geoffrey.

"Couldn't we all save up enough to buy him?" pleaded Helen.

Victoria said nothing, but the two tears ran down her face, and were followed by two more.

I looked at her, and gently wiped the tears away.

"I'll see what I can do," I said. "I'll ring up and find out how much they want for him—and whether they want to sell him straight away or not. We might be able to manage it later on. I'll get him for you if I can."

Victoria dried her eyes, and went down the big field with a pocket full of sugar. I left Helen in the garden with Christopher and Nicholas, and went to telephone.

When I came back I went to the gate of the big field and looked over. Victoria was cantering round the field on Snowy's bare back, her hair flying in the wind. When he slowed down she leant forward and put her arms round his neck.

I climbed over the gate and started to walk down the field. I still didn't know quite how I was going to manage it—but in the spring, Victoria could have her horse.

16

Safely Gathered In

That summer our garden really looked like a garden at last. The daffodils were followed by tulips, wallflowers, and forget-me-nots, and Steven and I sowed dozens of packets of seeds in one of the flower beds; later in the year we planted out hundreds of young plants.

On our hill-top we caught all the worst of the east winds, which, combined with our heavy clay soil, made everything in our garden several weeks later than it was in the valley below. But by late summer the garden was a glow of colour—the old rubbish dump covered again with golden nasturtiums, two long borders full of blue cornflowers and orange and yellow marigolds, the border along the side of the house brilliant with crimson and scarlet antirrhinums, and pink and red roses, clarkia, and purple larkspur and stocks in the other beds. The garden was filled with the scent of honeysuckle, lavender, stocks and roses, which spread into the house in the still evenings, with the scent of the corn, now golden and ripe, from the surrounding fields. Soon a massive red combine lumbered up through the drift into our front field, and in two days had cut all the fields round our house, while Helen helped the men to move the bales out of the way, and Christopher and Nicholas watched, fascinated, from our garden gate.

With nothing more to do in the garden, except cut the grass, until it was time to plant bulbs again, Steven suddenly decided he wanted to try making a cake.

It was a hot afternoon between summer and autumn when we got out the cookery book and started work. The first step was to shut the doors and windows and call all the cats out; the one drawback to our cats being that when we had any quantity of food out on the kitchen table, we had to keep them outside until it could be put under cover, which meant having all the doors and windows shut; and this, together with the oven on full on a hot day, did put the temperature up.

"I wish we could have a modern ventilation system installed," I said, as Steven spread the things he needed out on the table, "so we could get air in without having the windows open."

Victoria took Christopher and Nicholas out for a walk, and Geoffrey and Helen went out round the front of the house to play. Suddenly there was a crash of breaking glass. I ran through into the sitting-room.

"What's happened?"

Geoffrey came in the front door. "We've got a modern ventilation system now—like you said…" he announced.

A cool current of air drifted in, through the broken top half of one of the sitting-room windows.

"But what *happened?*" I still wanted to know.

Helen appeared contritely at the door. "I was shoo-ing a wasp out," she explained, "and I slipped…"

"So now," explained Geoffrey, "*we can* get air in without having to open the windows."

Well, for the time it did solve the problem of letting in coolness without cats—and we could have it replaced before the winter.

"But *don't* shoo any more wasps," I beseeched Helen. "We've got enough air now," and I went back to the kitchen.

"That's a lot cooler," said Steven cheerfully, hunting in one of the kitchen drawers. "Oh—*where* is the long-handled spoon?"

The long-handled spoon was really a pickle spoon, but we all believed it to have magic properties, since owing to its shape the bowl looked like a teaspoon and the handle looked like a des-sertspoon, so we could look straight at it, lying in the drawer with the other spoons, without seeing it, and consequently could never find it when we wanted it in a hurry.

"Take everything else out of the drawer," I advised him, "and it'll be the one that's left—look, there it is."

We settled down to work again. As time went on, I became increasingly convinced that cooking was Steven's true vocation; but I sometimes wished he had more of the instincts of a housewife. As I pointed out to him, the difference between the cook and the housewife is that the true cook works surrounded by an incredible muddle, concentrating only on the job in hand, and expecting someone else to clear up afterwards; while the average housewife learns from experience that this isn't practical in an ordinary household, and she keeps things clear all the way through. Steven, on the other hand, said that I frequently put away things which I knew quite well I should be wanting to use again in a few minutes' time…

Despite these differences of opinion, the cake was made and put in to cook, and telling Steven, "You can clear up—and don't forget the oven," I opened all the doors and windows again and went to meet Victoria and the weenybedes.

When we came back Steven had cleared up; and the cake was on the table. I put the kettle on the stove, and when it boiled we all sat down to tea.

The cake was excellent—"But I don't think it will keep," said Steven critically.

"No," I said, watching Geoffrey cutting himself a second slice, "I don't think it will."

And leaving the children to finish it, I went upstairs to give Carol her feed.

When autumn came I was still feeding Carol entirely myself, and she was nine months old. Reluctantly I decided that I ought to wean her, although I didn't really want to.

When it came to the point and I offered her cereal on a spoon, she decided she didn't want to be weaned either. She was very nice about it—no tears or protests—she even put out her tongue and felt the cereal on the spoon, to show she wasn't really unco-operative; she screwed up her mouth into a tight pink rose-bud, she smiled, she chuckled—but she just didn't get the idea of taking it into her mouth at all.

This didn't matter at the first try, or the second—but it went on day after day, with Carol still suckling happily and looking forward to the appearance of her cereal bowl as a new kind of game. I tried offering it before her feed, and I tried offering it after. It didn't make the slightest difference. Victoria tried, with the same result. Carol just didn't regard cereal as a meal.

Then I had an idea. Victoria held Carol on her lap and offered her the cereal, and as she held the spoon to her mouth, I put my arms round Carol and kissed her face. Obviously, Carol associated being kissed with having a meal—and she took the spoonful of cereal in. What was more, she swallowed it, although she looked rather surprised. And she took the next spoonful—and the next. She took every spoonful Victoria gave her, provided that I kissed each one in.

Then suddenly she decided that she liked cereal, and emptied the bowl, and looked round for more. Carol was weaned.

After that, feeding her appeared straightforward—but Carol was a young lady with ideas of her own. Being fed was pleasant, but not sufficiently interesting. She looked round for something else to do.

The first indication I had of her intentions was when she got hold of her feeding bowl with both hands, pulled it towards her, and put both feet in it. Removing one hand from a bowl of beef broth and spinach is messy enough; removing two hands and two feet simultaneously was too much for me. I did the next best thing, and removed the bowl—and called Victoria to help me clear up the mess.

When we had wiped most of the spinach off Carol and I picked up the bowl again, she was ready and waiting for it. I was too occupied in watching her feet to be on guard against her next move. Obviously, Carol thought this feeding business was too one-sided. She grabbed the spoon, as I lifted it, well-filled with spinach—and put it firmly into *my* mouth.

The trouble was that I didn't *like* spinach. So next time I carefully directed her hand, still firmly clasping the spoon, into her own mouth. Carol thought this was an excellent idea, and with my hand guiding hers, fed herself two spoonfuls. Then, just as I thought we were getting on nicely, she pulled the spoon away from me, scooped up a large load of spinach, and then, throwing out her hand, deposited most of the spinach in my hair.

I let Victoria feed her the rest of that meal; and she took it angelically, which was just as well, because Victoria didn't like spinach any more than I did. As it was, by the time Victoria and I had finished washing my hair, it was time for tea.

After that, Victoria and I took it in turns to feed Carol, since she was usually too interested in looking to see who it was to do anything more, for a little while at any rate. She became quite good at feeding herself; but we had to watch her feet all the time, as she still thought she ought to put them in the bowl. Sometimes I thought we might try letting her hold the spoon in her toes.

Then one day she thought of something quite new. We had just finished the meal, and I was scraping the bowl—fortunately—when she brought up both hands suddenly underneath it. The bowl flew up and landed upside-down on the side of her head. It was a pale blue plastic bowl, and she looked remarkably pretty in it, despite a blob of apple and custard on the tip of her nose.

But anyway, as I said to Victoria, it was comforting to know that, according to the books, we hadn't any feeding problem with her. Even as we were wiping the prune or the carrot out of our eyebrows, we had to admit that the really important thing had certainly been achieved.

17

Fire Overhead

Carol always thoroughly enjoyed her meals. It was not a hard winter that year, and although it rained continuously and our field was under flood again, there was practically no snow. We had paraffin fires in the sitting room, my bedroom (where Carol spent the day in her cot), and the weenybedes' bedroom; and when we wanted peace in the sitting room, Helen took Christopher and Nicholas up to their bedroom to play.

One morning, Victoria and I were doing the washing, Steven was out shopping, Geoffrey was studying in the sitting room, and Helen was playing with the weenybedes upstairs.

Suddenly there was a crash that shook the house, and a scream from Helen. Before I had got my hands out of the washing bowl, Geoffrey was halfway upstairs, and as I ran through into the sitting room he called down to me in a voice edged with panic, "The stove's fallen over! The room is on fire!"

I tore upstairs with Victoria behind me, calling to Geoffrey, "Get the babies out!" As I reached the landing, I passed Helen, looking very frightened, with Nicholas in her arms and Christopher holding on to her skirt, taking them downstairs.

In the doorway of the weenybedes' room I paused, facing a terrifying sight. The stove, a tall convector heater, had fallen forwards into the middle of the room, and the lid of the paraffin container inside must have been knocked off by the fall. Flames were leaping up all round the stove, while burning paraffin spread out over the floor.

It was a small room, and the curtains and bedding hung horrifyingly close to the flames. I had no fire extinguisher, and water would only float the burning paraffin. We needed sand—and had only mud.

"Quickly—get buckets of earth!" I called to the children. "The driest you can find—and bring the kitchen mat"—a hard cord one, now ingrained with dried mud, that was unlikely to catch fire. "I'll try to smother the flames. Hurry!"

Victoria and Helen brought the mat upstairs between them, while Geoffrey came back with a bucket of sodden earth in each hand. "There isn't any dryer than this," he said.

I took the buckets and threw the earth onto the flames. Even in the heat of the moment it occurred to me to feel a bit of a fool throwing mud down inside the house, when we normally spent so much time trying to keep it out.

The fire sizzled under the wet earth, but flames still flickered up all round it, and owing to the casing of the stove, I couldn't get the earth onto the source of the fire. Then I threw the mat over the stove, and the flames died down; but an ominous crackling under the mat made it clear that this had only caused a lull, and something else must be done without delay.

"I can't get at it properly," I said. "If only I could get the stove clear of the paraffin container, we might be able to smother it with earth..."

"Could you lift it off with the spade?" asked Geoffrey.

"Yes, I'll try," I said; and he ran to get the spade, while Victoria and Helen brought two more buckets of earth.

"I'll have to get in behind the stove," I said, when Geoffrey came back, "and lift it towards the door, away from the beds."

I edged my way into the room, until I was behind the stove with my back against the wall, while Geoffrey, Helen and Victoria watched from the landing. Then I pulled the mat away, and getting the spade under the stove I heaved it up, and it fell back with a clang on the floor. Immediately there was a roar and a sheet of flame leapt up in front of me, blocking my way to the door.

"Look, the curtains are on fire!" cried Helen.

Somehow I managed to beat them out with my hands. The fire was still blazing between me and the door, and as I stood pressed against the farthest wall I could feel the heat of the flames terrifyingly close to my face.

"Get out, quickly!" cried Geoffrey.

"I can't!" I said. "Throw that earth on the fire and try to get the flames down…"

"What about the window?" Geoffrey called, as he emptied the two buckets on to the flames. "Could you climb out?"

I moved towards the window, but a tongue of flame caught the hem of my skirt, and I stepped back. Helen and Victoria were crying now, and I wasn't sure how much longer my legs would hold up…

"You must get out!" Geoffrey almost sobbed. "The whole room will be on fire in a minute!"

"All right—I'll try," I said, and fighting back panic I held my skirt up and jumped through the flames to the door. It was over in a second, and I was on the other side. The fire crackled and blazed behind me.

I turned and looked back into the room. The linoleum was on fire now, and the flames were spreading rapidly.

"Get the babies out, quickly!" I cried. "We may have to abandon the house…"

I don't remember clearly what happened after that. The children told me afterwards that I ran downstairs and fetched a bucket of water, but I have no recollection of doing so whatever, although I do remember passing Victoria somewhere with Carol in her arms. And I remember standing in the doorway of the blazing room and throwing the bucket of water into the flames.

There was a loud hissing, and a lot of black smoke; and then it was all over. The paraffin had burnt itself out, and my bucket of water had extinguished the burning linoleum. Only smoking, scorched patches on the floor, and the battered and blackened stove remained.

My legs gave way then, and I don't remember anything else until I found I was lying on the landing, and Geoffrey was bending over me holding a glass of water and sobbing hysterically. I sat up and took the water, and assured him that I was alive and unhurt, and had only fainted.

When I went into my bedroom I had another shock, for Carol's cot was empty, and I had forgotten seeing Victoria carrying her out.

"It's all right—I took her downstairs," Victoria explained. "She's quite happy on the settee with the weenybedes, and Helen is looking after them. I'll go and bring her back if you're all right now."

At this point Steven came back, laden with groceries, and gazed in astonishment at our exhausted and blackened figures, and the weenybedes' room with piles of mud all over the floor.

"Whatever's been happening?" he asked.

"We had a fire," I explained weakly.

"Oh," said Steven. And then with dawning horror, "Who's got to clear up the mess?"

"We thought *you* might," said Geoffrey cheerfully, but he was still very white round the mouth.

"I thought so," said Steven resignedly.

"Look," I said. "Geoffrey, I think you'd better go and lie down for a bit; Steven and Helen, will you start clearing up here—shovel up the earth into buckets, to start with, and take it back to the garden—and get the stove downstairs—perhaps you could help them with that, Geoffrey, if it's cool enough to handle yet. I don't know if it will ever work again. Victoria, come down with me and look after the weenybedes, while I get lunch and finish the washing."

So we put Carol, delighted with all the excitement, back in her cot; and started putting the day back in order again.

Geoffrey carried the stove downstairs into the kitchen, and then went to lie down in his room; when I went to look at him a few minutes later he was sound asleep. Steven and Helen started clearing up the weenybedes' room, and somehow there seemed to be a lot more earth to clear out than we had carried in.

After about an hour I had finished the washing, and lunch was cooking, and Victoria was feeding the weenybedes; and Geoffrey came downstairs, his normal colour back in his face, and started trying to get the stove into working order again.

I went up to feed Carol, and dared to look at the clearing up operations. Steven and Helen were scrubbing the floor, and all traces of the fire, excepting the blackened patches on the linoleum, had disappeared.

"It looks better now, doesn't it?" said Steven. "But how did it happen? Helen won't tell me."

"How *did* it happen, Helen?" I inquired pointedly.

Helen looked guilty. "I was sitting on the window sill behind the stove, with Christopher and Nicholas," she said, "and I put my feet on the stove to warm them—and then I got up quickly, and the stove just fell over."

"I see," I said.

"We were playing a game," explained Helen.

"Well—don't," I said. "Don't play any more games with your feet on a lighted oil stove—you and the babies might have been burned to death."

"I got them out quickly," said Helen, looking distressed.

"You nearly got us *all* out quickly," I said. "Never mind, it's over now, but don't play games on a fire again.—You've cleared it up beautifully now, anyway."

When I went down again Geoffrey looked up from the stove and said, "It looks a mess, but I think I can get it to work. The handles have come off the paraffin container—solder melted in the heat, I suppose—and it seems to be leaking a bit, but not enough to lose much. We can get that mended, anyway. I'll pull the wick up and see if I can get it to light."

Lifting the wick was a long and messy operation, since most of it had been burnt away, but at last everything was back in place.

When I went into the kitchen to serve out lunch I found Geoffrey sitting crossly in front of the stove with a half-empty matchbox in his hand, and a litter of burnt-out matches scattered round him on the floor.

"I *can't* get it to light," he said in an agonized voice. And then, "Ah, wait a minute—I think that's done it."

A thin flicker of blue flame spread slowly round the battered wick.

"Got it!" said Geoffrey triumphantly. "You wouldn't think it would be so difficult to light."

Then he caught my eye, and we both laughed.

18

Beware of the Bull

As our second winter passed, the weenybedes went on growing, and in the beginning of the New Year they all had birthdays; first Nicholas, who was two; then Carol, who was one; and a week later Christopher, who was three. Carol didn't know she was having a birthday; but Christopher and Nicholas shared a birthday cake, of which the two candles pleased them more than anything else, and Nicholas had a push-horse and Christopher a tricycle, both of which for several weeks they insisted on taking to bed with them every night.

Carol grew daily more adorable, and was beginning to crawl—or rather, like Nicholas at the same age, to wriggle and push herself towards anything she wanted whenever she was put on the floor. She still hadn't even one tooth through, although she seemed to be trying hard; but she had grown very pretty, with big blue eyes and dark lashes, and her pale golden-brown hair was long and softly curling, falling in a tangle to her shoulders, and in a frilly curtain over her face. Nothing we could do would persuade her to keep a slide or a ribbon on it for more than a few minutes; as soon as we secured the hair back out of her eyes, she put up her hands and pulled the ribbon or slide out and threw it away. So she went on looking out at the world from under her frilly curtain, pushing it aside with the back of her hand whenever she encountered something she particularly wanted to see.

She also objected to wearing clothes and nappies, and soon learned to take these off too. Woolly jackets she pulled off over her head, as she couldn't undo the buttons; and invariably, when

I came to dress her in the mornings, I found she had taken her nightdress off, and pulled her legs out of her nappies, which, held only by the pin to her vest, trailed like a train behind her.

She seldom cried in the night, despite the—presumably—coming teeth, and when she did cry I had only to say softly, "Carol—sweet Carol," a few times and she would go back to sleep without my even having to get out of bed.

We all adored her; including Christopher and Nicholas, who ran into my bedroom whenever they found the door open, and often climbed into her cot to play with her, kiss her, and comfort her when she cried. She carried on long "conversations" with them, and it seemed likely that she would learn to talk before Nicholas; already she joined in calling "Ayo! Ayo!" when she saw them coming, and "Awa! Awa!"—the weenybede word for good night or good-bye.

Christopher particularly loved her, and took the responsibility of being an elder brother seriously, despite the small difference in their actual ages. He couldn't say "Carol" properly, so he called her "Tugar"—weenybede for Sugar—and if he heard her crying and couldn't get her to stop, he would run to me or Victoria calling urgently, "Come quickly and make Tugar happy!"

Nicholas continued to say "No!" and no amount of persuasion could induce him to say "Yes." We tried hard, but with his head on one side and his blue eyes full of laughter, he would parry every attempt —

"Nicholas—do you like cream?"

"Creeeeem…!"

"Do you like chocolate?"

"More!"

And then as a last hope—"Do you like me?" to which he responded with a long sweet kiss and murmured against my face, "Do-oo…"

He also invented a phrase the meaning of which we never did discover, since he used it for everything he wanted, and caused us endless speculation as to its origin—Doo wun. Geoffrey said at first it meant "Blue one," and I believed it was "New one," and Victoria said he meant he wanted to "Do one"—but Nicholas went on saying Doo wun, with great insistence, and in the end we gave it up and decided it was just Nicholas-ese.

A literally growing problem with Nicholas was his hair. It was thick, long and curly, and he resisted with increasing strength and violence all our attempts to cut it short. Despite Victoria's efforts to distract his attention, he tried to climb down out of the high chair as soon as I started cutting, and had to be held back, struggling, while I clipped any bit of hair that came within range. He yelled so loudly that he even objected to the noise himself, and put his hands over his ears.

As soon as it was over he recovered his usual cheerfulness, but the mere sight of the scissors produced shrieks of protest, and as my reactions were becoming rather similar—his hair seemed to have the consistency of wire-netting, and clipping it made my fingers sore—we decided to abandon our attempts to shear this very unwilling Samson, and only try to keep the ends trimmed, whenever he could be held still for long enough, to prevent its falling right over his face. I did sometimes wonder whether it might be possible to cut it when he was asleep.

There was great excitement among the weenybedes when Carol came downstairs into the playroom. Our old playpen was completely dismantled by now, so I bought Carol a new one, with a floor to it, and installed it in the playroom and Carol inside. Both Christopher and Nicholas, who had protested continuously against the restriction of their own playpen days, immediately climbed in too, and we might have had a long period of unusual peace and quiet; only Carol after a time grew tired of the playpen, so while Christopher and Nicholas played happily in it, she had to come out and practise dry-land swimming—her latest method of crawling—on the sitting-room floor.

At the end of the winter the weather was mild, and when the house was quiet we could hear the bleating of new-born lambs on the surrounding fields. Geoffrey and Victoria went to see them, and Victoria took Christopher, but he was as apprehensive as they were at first, and while the lambs retreated behind their mothers, he watched them from behind Victoria's skirt...

"Me saw sheep," he announced when he came back, and added in a puzzled voice, "Sheep all wool!"

The mare and foal and the ponies had been taken away at the beginning of the winter, but there were now three racehorses, two golden brown and one dark grey, turned out on the big field behind the house. Victoria and Helen spent most of their spare time with them, feeding them with apples and sugar, until the horses used to wait at the gate for them to come. They named them Starlight, Lightning and Moonlight; and before long Victoria was riding the grey one, Moonlight, bareback round the field.

"He's lonely," she said. "He always stands by himself at the bottom of the field—the other horses won't have him with them because he's such an odd colour."

When our landlord got to hear of it he was horrified, and came to see me in great agitation.

"Your girls have got to stop riding that grey horse!" he began.

"I'm sorry," I said. "I didn't think it could do any harm to the horse."

"To the *horse!*" he exploded. "That horse isn't safe to go near, let alone for a child to ride! It's already thrown one man and broken his leg!"

But Victoria took this calmly. "He's been ill-treated by someone I think, and the other horses don't like him, so he gets snappy. He won't hurt me—he likes me," she said.

Keeping Victoria away from horses is like keeping wasps away from a jar of honey, so I accepted the inevitable, and Victoria continued to play with Moonlight and ride him round the field. He never attempted to throw her off, regarding her with evident affection, and in fact I lived in increasing apprehension that I might one day find him, like the carthorse, established in the garden, waiting for sugar at the kitchen door.

Everywhere now activity began to waken round us, and the weenybedes came in from walks bursting with excitement about the things they'd seen.

One afternoon Christopher rushed in from fetching the milk with Steven and Helen.

"*Two* lorries!" he told us. "On our road—dropping stones!"

"They're making up the road at the bottom of the drift," explained Steven.

"Are the lorries still there?" Geoffrey asked Christopher.

"No—have tea now," said Christopher.

"The lorries have tea?" Geoffrey teased him.

But Christopher had not only a vivid imagination but a very literal mind.

"Of course not!" he replied indignantly. "Lorries not eat—the men does it!" He ran to Victoria. "Me is hungry!" he announced. "Get my tea!"

"Has the butter come?" I asked. Our butter is delivered with the milk.

"Yes—Helen and Nicholas are bringing it," said Steven.

At that moment Helen came in the door, pushing Nicholas in his chair.

"Where's the butter?" asked Victoria.

"Nicholas has it," said Helen. She retrieved an odd-shaped object wrapped up in paper.

"Is that the butter?" asked Geoffrey incredulously. "What happened to it?"

"I gave it to Nicholas to hold," explained Helen, "and I think he sat on it."

"That's what it looks like," said Steven.

We unwrapped the butter and restored it to more or less its original shape, and started getting the weenybedes' tea. The next day Christopher ran in from the garden, calling, "Look! More lorry—up our field!"

We went to see, and there was a large cattle float coming up. It went on up the back loke, and on the field half-way up the loke unloaded several black cows and calves—and a large, black bull.

I watched the departure of the cattle float rather apprehensively.

"I hope that fence is secure!" said Geoffrey, voicing my thoughts.

"We'd better keep the babies away from the loke," I said. "He looked quiet enough, but you never know what bulls are going to do."

A few days later I had to go into the town, and walked up the back loke on my way to the train.

It was nearly dark when I came back, and Geoffrey came to the station to meet me. As we reached the top of the loke I said, "I hope the bull doesn't get out. I shouldn't like to meet him in the middle of the loke in the dark."

We started walking down the rutted lane, darkened by the overhanging trees and hedges. Suddenly I stopped and pointed ahead in horror.

"Geoffrey—look!"

Standing in our path, facing us, was a large black shape—and as we stopped short it uttered a loud "Moooo!"

It was several minutes before I realized that it was one of the little black calves…

Standing in the half-light it looked enormous. But it moooo'd again, plaintively, and we realized that it was lost and frightened, and probably missing its mother.

"We ought to put it back on the field," said Geoffrey.

"So long as the bull doesn't get out when we open the gate," I said.

We walked slowly down the loke towards the calf, which turned hastily and started to run ahead of us.

"It's frightened," I said. "One of us ought to get ahead of it, and stop it going past the gate—it might go on down our field and out on to the road."

"I'll try to get past it over the fields," said Geoffrey, putting down the parcels he was carrying.

He scrambled through the hedge, and then I heard him running along on the other side. After a few minutes his voice came out of the darkness ahead.

"All right—drive it down slowly now."

I walked on, leaving my parcels behind too, and trying to keep the calf in sight without frightening it into charging past Geoffrey, who was still out of sight ahead.

At last we came to the gate of the field where the cattle were, and Geoffrey, appearing out of the darkness beyond, cautiously opened the gate. We could see nothing of the other cattle on the field, but we couldn't be sure whether they were there or not, because black cows don't show up very well in the dark. I watched the open gate with growing nervousness, as the calf showed its obvious intention of going anywhere except through it and back into the field.

"Don't frighten it!" urged Geoffrey anxiously.

"Couldn't you tell it not to frighten me?" I suggested, as the calf made a sudden rush in my direction. "And the bull too, if he's anywhere near."

The calf dodged to one side unexpectedly, and I dived in front of it again. It turned, looked hopefully round for some other opening, suddenly saw the field lying beyond, and went at a run through the gate.

"Good!" said Geoffrey. "I wonder where it got out?"

"Does it matter now?" I started, when a thought struck me. "Perhaps it does, though. Where a calf can get out, there must be a gap, and where there's a gap—"

"A bull can get through," agreed Geoffrey.

"But we'll never find anything in the dark," I said.

"It may be where the wire runs across the pond in the corner of the field," said Geoffrey. "They've pushed that aside before."

So we walked on down the loke to the corner of the field, and started examining the wires across the pond; and we soon found that Geoffrey was right. Two strands of barbed wire had been pushed apart at the far side, leaving a gap that anything could get through.

"Can you get round the other side and lift it, while I pull it taut?" Geoffrey asked.

Cautiously I climbed through into the field, and crept round the pond. Balancing myself on the bank, I hauled on the wire. Geoffrey pulled hard, and twisted it back round its support.

"Right, that's done it," he said, rubbing his hands where the wire had grazed them. "Horrid stuff, barbed wire. Can you get back?"

"I think so," I said.

I leapt back from the muddy bank of the pond into the field. As I landed another large black shape moved in the darkness in front of me. I gave it a push and it lumbered away.

Geoffrey shouted, "Ho, ho," and I heard the feet of many cattle retreating. Breathlessly I rejoined him on the other side of the fence.

"They must have been round the pond all the time," said Geoffrey.

"Yes, I know," I said. "I landed at the feet of one of the cows when I jumped off the bank."

"No, you didn't," said Geoffrey, chuckling. "That was the bull."

We collected our parcels from up the loke, and went on back to the house.

19

Bringing Down the House

With spring really on the way, we decided to make an early start on our spring cleaning, to get it over before the longer and warmer days ahead. We started with the bedrooms; first mine, and then the weenybedes' room and the children's rooms; and then the landing and stairs. Steven washed floors, Geoffrey beat carpets and curtains on the line, Victoria and Helen and I washed woodwork and polished furniture; and by the end of a week we had the upstairs done.

One evening a few days later, we were all in the sitting-room, while Victoria and I bathed the weenybedes. Carol was already in her cot, and I finished Nicholas and carried him upstairs, while Victoria started on Christopher.

I put Nicholas into his cot, kissed him good night, tucked him in, and went downstairs again. I had only been in the sitting-room for a few minutes when there was a sickening, rending crash from upstairs. It was the sort of noise that I remembered hearing many years ago—during the War. Immediately afterwards Nicholas started to cry.

We all ran upstairs, Steven, who was nearest, leading the way, into the weenybedes' room.

The room was thick with dust, and lumps of plaster covered the floor. More plaster hung from the gaping rafters overhead. The ceiling on one side of the room had fallen down.

Nicholas, covered with dust and crying frantically, was sitting up in his cot holding up his arms to be rescued. But he was unhurt. The bulk of the plaster had fallen by the side of the cot —exactly where I had been standing when I said good night to him, about two minutes before.

I picked Nicholas up and carried him downstairs. He was very frightened, and I sat down in the settee with him in my arms.

"What are we going to do?" asked Steven, and Victoria added, "Where will the weenybedes sleep tonight?"

"There isn't anywhere else they *can* sleep," I said. "We'll have to try to clean up the room. Steven and Helen, will you see what you can do—get the furniture out of the room and shake out all the bedding, and sweep up the plaster. Geoffrey, you could help them to move the furniture."

"What shall we do with the plaster?" Helen wanted to know.

"Carry it out in buckets," I said.

The three of them went upstairs, and Victoria got Christopher out of his bath, while I comforted Nicholas, washed his face and hands again, shook out his pyjamas, and combed the plaster out of his hair.

Soon Geoffrey came downstairs, to report that they had got all the furniture out and Helen was washing it; and Steven followed, with the first bucket of plaster.

"I seem to have done this before," he grumbled, carrying it out of the back door.

"Could it have been the fire that damaged the plaster?" asked Geoffrey.

"I don't know," I said. "It didn't show any signs of coming down—it wasn't even cracked."

"Perhaps we loosened it when we were sweeping the ceiling," suggested Victoria.

"Oh dear—our spring cleaning!" I mourned. "All that plaster dust over everything!"

Steven appeared with another full bucket.

"What shall I do?" he asked, "because there's a lot of plaster hanging down from the ceiling, and a lot more that's loose that will come down if you touch it, and it won't be any good putting the babies back to bed with more plaster likely to fall on them during the night."

"I'll come up and look," I said.

I left Nicholas, now smiling again, sitting on the settee with Christopher, who was by now in his pyjamas, while Victoria got them both a drink of warm, sweet milk.

Even viewed by candlelight, the room presented a most depressing sight. The dust still lay thick on the floor, and the dank smell of the plaster filled the air. Lumps of plaster hung from the hole in the ceiling, and cracks and bulges appeared all round it. Black cobwebs, heavy with the dust of ages, dangled through the broken rafters.

"I think the only thing we *can* do is to strip the lot," I said. "Get everything that will move out of the room—take down the curtains and the lampshade and everything. And then get in here with a broom and shut the door, and knock down every piece of plaster that will come, and sweep the rafters clear. That should make it safe for tonight, at any rate. You might use the hoe to do the knocking down—you'd better do it, Steven, because you've got the shortest hair."

"And then I'll clear up all the mess," said Helen cheerfully.

"Come on, Helen, let's get the hoe," said Steven, running downstairs.

"Geoffrey, will you take all the bedding and curtains out, and put them over the line and beat them—and bring them in when the others have finished," I said, and I went downstairs again to Victoria and the weenybedes.

Victoria and I took Christopher and Nicholas on to our laps to reassure them, while Geoffrey went out with armfuls of blankets and curtains, and a violent banging and thudding upstairs told us that Steven had started work.

"Put some water on to heat, Geoffrey," I said, when he came in again. "I'll have to wash Steven's hair, and Helen's. And I think they'd better have a bath, too, by the time they've done."

"I'd better fill the copper then," said Geoffrey. "Is there a spare bucket?"

He found one and started carrying in buckets of soft water.

Nicholas was nearly asleep in my arms, while Christopher sat looking at a book and every few minutes rubbing his eyes and yawning. Still the banging and thumping went on overhead.

After a time I said to Geoffrey, "Go up and see how far they've got—but *don't* open the door."

Geoffrey went up and called through the door to Steven, and came down to report that he wanted me to come up and see what he'd done.

I tied an old cot sheet round my head and went cautiously in. The room was still thick with dust, and plaster lay ankle deep on the floor. All that was left of the ceiling was a strip of firm plaster over Christopher's bed—the rest was bare rafters.

"I couldn't get that down," said Steven, pointing to the remaining strip of plaster. "I've banged it as hard as I could, but it won't move, so I shouldn't think it's likely to fall tonight."

"And I've swept down all the cobwebs that were coming through," said Helen, shuddering. "Now we'd better start on the floor, hadn't we?"

"Yes—do the best you can with it," I said. "Geoffrey can help you carry the plaster out. You've made a good job of the ceiling, Steven. And there'll be baths ready for you as soon as you've finished."

I went down and started getting supper, while Steven and Geoffrey carried out bucket after bucket of plaster, and Helen fetched a bucket of hot soapy water and a scrubbing brush, and took it upstairs. At last they had got the plaster clear, and Steven and Helen started washing the walls and scrubbing the floor.

By the time they had finished, supper was ready, and both the weenybedes were asleep on the settee, so while Steven and Helen bathed, Victoria and I went up and got the furniture back, with Geoffrey's help, and made up the bed and cot again. Despite the open window, the smell of plaster still hung in the air. The broken ceiling looked dark and rather frightening, and I was glad that Christopher and Nicholas wouldn't be able to see it until the morning.

Victoria and I carried the weenybedes up and tucked them in. Although their bed-clothes had been thoroughly shaken out, the blankets still felt sticky with plaster dust. But they didn't wake, and we crept out and left them at last to sleep. It was eleven o'clock.

I went down and washed Steven's and Helen's hair, and it was so thick with plaster dust that the first waters I used were literally muddy. It was midnight before we had supper and went to bed.

The next morning I went in early to the weenybedes. The wind had got up in the night, and there was now half a gale blowing. I shivered as I stood in the now too-well-ventilated room...

Nicholas was still asleep, but Christopher was sitting up, looking at the ceiling over his head with astonishment.

"What *that* is?" he wanted to know, pointing at the rafters. "What that there *for?*"

Seen in daylight, the ceiling looked worse than it had the night before. Up above the rafters, more cobwebs hung—black and hairy—and beyond them patches of sky were visible, where dislodged tiles let the daylight through. I could clearly hear birds chirping and hopping about in the roof.

Shutting the window, I called Victoria to help me get the weenybedes quickly dressed and downstairs into the warmth of the rooms below.

As I moved about the house, it soon became apparent that the dust of the plaster had spread everywhere. It lay thick on the woodwork of the stairs and landing; the carpets were impregnated with it; a film of dust had penetrated even through the doors into the other bedrooms, and the sitting-room and playroom downstairs.

"I hope there aren't any more ceilings about to come down," said Steven at breakfast.

"Well, mine can't," I said cheerfully, "because it was down when I first saw the house, and the builders put up ceiling boards, not plaster. And I don't think yours or the girls' will, because of the beams going across and holding it up."

"There are a lot of cracks in the kitchen ceiling," said Helen.

"There are a lot of cracks everywhere, when you come to look at it," said Geoffrey. "The plaster is coming away from the walls in several places—in the playroom, and the weenybedes' room, and behind the settee."

This was quite true—we had kept patching them up, but nothing would stick on the plaster, and I hadn't felt like facing the upheaval of having builders in when there was so little space for all of us already.

"What shall we do about the weenybedes' ceiling?" asked Victoria.

"I don't know," I said. "I suppose we shall have to have boards put up, like they did in my room—but how we're going to manage with builders in the house and the weenybedes' room out of use, I don't know."

"Couldn't we do it ourselves?" asked Geoffrey.

"Could you?" I countered.

"I could try," said Geoffrey.

"Couldn't we move somewhere else while we have the repairs done?" asked Steven.

"Where?" I said. "Do you think Anna and Danilo would make room for us all in their wardrobe for a week or so?"

"If we wait until the summer, we could have a tent on the lawn," said Helen hopefully.

We all went up and looked at the ceiling again, but it didn't seem to make the problem any easier.

When we came down, Steven said, "Did you know there was a rose growing through the sitting-room window?"

"Where?" I said, startled.

He was quite right. We had mended the window that Helen had broken the previous autumn with Windolite, but somehow a shoot of the rambler rose growing outside had pushed its way through, and was now showing an inch of budding leaves inside the room.

"Well—leave it for a bit," I said. "It would be rather nice if it flowered."

"If we're going to have some repairs done, what about the catch on our door?" asked Geoffrey.

The catch on the outside of their door had broken some months before, and we had made a temporary repair with a piece of string—attached to the catch inside the room, leading over the top of the door, and tied to the handle outside—which we pulled to lift the latch. This worked so well that we were apt to forget about it, except on the periodic occasions when the string broke and we found ourselves shut out, and Geoffrey or Steven had to climb in at the window to open the door.

"And there's the latch on the sitting-room door, too," said Helen. "We're still using a tea-spoon to open that."

"Have you noticed the back door frame recently?" I asked.

"Every time the door is shut it pulls it out, and it's slowly coming away from the wall."

"We might have something done about the bathroom wall, too," said Geoffrey thoughtfully.

The bathroom wall had always been inexplicably damp, but being the bathroom it never seemed to matter very much, and anyway I wasn't sure what we could do about it.

"It looks as if the bricks needed pointing," I said, "but that was done before we moved in."

"Perhaps the bricks themselves have become porous," said Geoffrey. "They must be very old bricks, after all."

"Well, that would mean having the whole wall re-built," I said.

"We can't do that," objected Steven. "We've got jasmin and Virginia creeper growing up that wall."

"Now we've got Carol, we really need another room," said Victoria. "Couldn't we have one built on?"

"It would be a help," I said. "But have you noticed the cracks in the tiles over the weenybedes' ceiling? We've never had any water through there, not even in the snow, but I wonder how long it's going to last?"

There was a sudden crash from upstairs.

"Oh, what is it *now*?" I cried.

"It sounded like a window," said Geoffrey.

It was. The landing window, left uncatched, had been caught by a sudden gust of wind, and blown out—smashing the glass against the wall.

"We'll have to cover that with something, quickly," I said. "There's a draught cutting through the whole house now."

We came back to the breakfast table, and looked at each other.

"The entire house seems to be disintegrating," I said despairingly.

"Well—the floors are solid enough," said Geoffrey.

"*And* damp—the linoleum keeps rotting and tearing away," I said. "The bricks are only laid on the earth, after all."

"Well, the earth is solid, anyway!" said Geoffrey.

"If out of the whole house, all we've got left in a reasonable state of repair is the earth—" I burst out.

"And the sky!" said Victoria. "Christopher and Nicholas can

see the sky now through their ceiling. They can watch the birds flying over as they lie in bed."

"And it will be lovely and cool in the summer," said Helen, but rather doubtfully.

"It's lovely and cool now," I said, shivering. "Go and see what you can do with that window, Geoffrey. And then we'll get the house cleaned through—that's all we can do today, anyway."

"But what shall we do about the ceiling?" persisted Geoffrey.

"We'll deal with today first, and worry about tomorrow when we come to it," I said.

"You always say that," said Steven.

"I know," I said. "That's why my hair hasn't turned white yet."

And we set about dealing with the day.

20

On With the Show

Spring came early that year, warm and damp like a new baby. The cuckoo called over the fields again, and the swallows came back, with a flash of dark-blue wings over the young green wheat, to their old nest in the barn. A pigeon nested there too, on one of the high beams, and Christopher and Nicholas went every morning to look at the nest, where they could see the parent bird's head showing over the edge.

The banks of the loke were creamy with cow-parsley, and cowslips shone like sunbeams in the grass. In our garden, the daffodils faded, giving way to the tulips and forget-me-nots and mauve aubretia, and brilliant crimson and violet anemones. The pear tree was heavy with white blossom, filled all day with the humming of bees, and the buds on the apple trees showed rose pink in the increasing warmth of the sun.

The moorhens that nested on the pond hatched out a family of six young ones, like small black powder-puffs, and Victoria spent hours lying under the bushes on the bank of the pond, watching them swimming in the still green water below. Steven and Helen went out every evening picking hogweed for the rabbits; Anna and Danilo were again expecting young, and so were two of their offspring of the previous year. Steven went round the local shops and brought back two orange boxes—one at a time, balanced precariously on the handle-bars of his bicycle—to make into another hutch for their increasing families.

We moved Carol's playpen into the garden, and Christopher and Nicholas played outside all day. Christopher rode his tricycle, and Nicholas his push-horse, and Christopher started trying to climb the apple trees; and they both picked handfuls of flowers and brought them to Carol or Victoria or me. Our cats lay in the grass blinking sleepily in the sun, and only moved when Christopher nearly ran over them as he cycled round the lawn. Victoria and I did the washing outside, and Geoffrey spent his spare time helping to hoe sugar beet at the farm.

The one thing we could never achieve, because of the weenybedes and the number of us all, was a week's holiday. But now Carol was weaned, and the summer too arrived early and looked like being even hotter than the previous year, I thought we should be able to manage days out—if not for all of us at once, at least one at a time for everyone.

First, Victoria wanted to go to a horse show, to be held at a village over fifty miles away. I didn't feel that I could take her myself and leave all the weenybedes to Helen for a whole day; but I could take Geoffrey, before the day of the show, leaving the weenybedes with Victoria, and show him where to go; and when the day came, he could—and did—take Victoria to the show.

They set off early in the morning and arrived back late in the evening, Victoria ecstatic after spending the whole afternoon watching horses, and everything having gone according to plan.

So when they all wanted to go to the County Show, only ten miles away, I didn't see why that couldn't be arranged too. They knew the location of the showground, for we passed it when we went by bus to our main town, so there would be no difficulty about their finding their way. Geoffrey, Steven, and Victoria all wanted to go; in the end Helen decided she would rather have a day by the sea with me, so she stayed at home on Show day to help me look after the weenybedes.

The three elder children set off first thing in the morning, with a picnic lunch and definite instructions about not separating without arranging a meeting-place first, as Geoffrey wanted to spend some of the time looking round the showground, while Victoria and Steven preferred to see all the events in the ring. Helen and I and the weenybedes settled down together to a quiet day.

The others were due back at about eight-thirty, and by then

Helen and I had got the babies into bed and cleared up, and I was doing the ironing. I had just finished the last nappy when Geoffrey walked in—alone.

As soon as I looked at his face, I knew there was something wrong.

"Where are the others?" I asked him.

"I lost them," he said. His mouth trembled. "They were listening to the band, and I arranged to meet them there just before it was time for the bus, but when I came back they weren't there—and then I thought they must have missed me and gone straight to the bus stop, like you said, so I went out to the bus stop, but they weren't there either—and then the bus came, and I thought I'd better come back, as otherwise you wouldn't know what had happened to us—so I came without them..." He broke off and looked at me miserably. "I did try to find them..."

I was conscious of rising panic, but knew I mustn't show it; Geoffrey was frightened enough already.

"You did quite right," I reassured him. "If you hadn't come back, I would have been terribly worried and wouldn't have known what to do. Do you know what time the next bus is coming back?"

We looked it up—it was not for another two hours.

"Well, assuming they're all right, they can't get back until half-past ten," I said. "But if anything *has* happened to them—it's no good waiting until then to see if they come—it would be too late to do anything then. I think we'd better try to find them straight away, in case."

"How?" asked Geoffrey, rather desperately.

"I think we ought to notify the police," I said slowly. "It can't do any harm, and if anything is wrong—" (but I dared not let myself think of what might have happened) "—the police are the right people to deal with it. But I expect they just went off and got interested in something else, and forgot about the bus—you know how dreamy Steven is. Don't worry—it's not really likely that anything would happen to them in a crowd of people like that."

I hadn't quite managed to convince myself, and I couldn't stop thinking of the stretches of unfrequented woodland surrounding the showground—but Geoffrey looked relieved.

"There's acres of the Show, and they might have been anywhere in it," he said. "I couldn't look very far for them, because it was time for the bus."

At that moment Helen came in, her arms full of hogweed for the rabbits.

"What's happened? Where are Steven and Victoria?" she demanded, seeing Geoffrey's tense face.

"They've got lost," I told her. "They didn't meet Geoffrey as they'd arranged, so he had to come back without them. They'll probably be on the next bus, but it doesn't get in until half-past ten. We're just deciding what best to do."

I turned to Geoffrey again.

"I think you'd better telephone the police," I told him, "because you can tell them exactly what happened—and give them a description of Steven and Victoria, and what they were wearing—they can't miss Victoria's hair—" …but my heart faltered with a sudden horrifying vision of that golden hair lying in some thicket and Victoria cold and still.

"Right—I'll go now," said Geoffrey, and set off on his bicycle down the field.

Helen turned to me with a frightened face.

"What's happened to them? What do you want the police to do?"

"I don't expect anything has happened," I said, hoping my face didn't show all I felt. "But we're going to ask the police to look for them, just to make sure they're all right."

I started putting away the ironing and looking every few minutes towards the door. Helen kept unnaturally quiet, watching me.

"If anything *had* happened, the police would come to tell us," I said at last. "So if no one comes, they're almost certainly all right."

The sound of the door made us both jump—but it was Geoffrey back from the telephone.

"I told them," he said. "They hadn't heard anything, and they took full details of their clothes and everything. Victoria's hair is done in a pony-tail, isn't it? And they're going to contact the showground right away."

"Will a policeman go and look for them?" asked Helen.

"I expect they'll telephone the police at the Show, and they'll search," I said.

"And broadcast a description over the showground loudspeakers, probably," said Geoffrey. "They made several announcements about articles that had been lost or found, while we were there—and children who were lost too."

It was a still, warm evening, and the house seemed suddenly oppressive. We went outside and sat on the grass by the gate. "Won't Steven and Victoria be surprised when they know the police are looking for them!" said Helen.

"Well, there's nothing else we can do now," I said, "except wait. Until this happened, did you enjoy the Show, Geoffrey?"

"Oh, yes," he said, brightening. "The others got seats by the show ring straight away, and I stayed with them to see some of the events, and we had lunch together—and then I left them and looked round the stands. There were sheepdog trials, and the musical ride by the Mounted Police, and on one of the stands there were milking machines and the man showed me how to work one, and I saw a combine like Mr. Potter's, only a newer design. I looked round for about an hour, and then I went back to the ring, and we all went and had tea. It was after that they wanted to listen to the band, and I arranged to meet them."

His face clouded again. I looked at my watch. It was half-past nine.

"They can't be back for another hour at least," I said. "And then they'll have to cycle from the bus stop."

It was starting to grow colder, so we went indoors again.

"Perhaps I could go to the bus stop to meet them," suggested Geoffrey.

"That's a good idea," I said.

At ten o'clock he left, and Helen and I were alone. She sat very still on an upright chair, and when I next looked at her I saw she was crying.

"Don't worry, Helen darling," I said, but I felt very near to tears myself. Of course nothing *had* happened to them, but—supposing something had, after all?

I sat down on the settee with Helen in my arms. Slowly the hands of the clock moved on…

Half-past ten… "The bus should be just coming in," I told Helen. "We'll soon know now."

At a quarter to eleven I started going to the landing window and looking out. Helen went and stood by the garden gate.

Then, as I went to the window for about the tenth time, I saw the light of a bicycle coming up the field—and another, and another…

"It's all right—I think!" I called down to Helen. "There are three bicycles coming up the field!"

I ran down and out of the door to meet them. Victoria, Steven and Geoffrey were getting off their bicycles at the gate.

"They *were* on the bus," said Geoffrey.

I demanded, "Steven, Victoria, what happened to you?—why weren't you on the first bus?"

"We forgot," said Victoria.

"We stayed by the band until it finished, and then we walked round waiting for Geoffrey, but he didn't come," said Steven.

"I came to where I'd left you, as we'd arranged," exploded Geoffrey.

"I don't know how you missed us," said Steven indignantly.

"You should have stayed in exactly the same place, Steven—I did tell you," I said. "You've worried us all dreadfully—did the police find you in the end?"

"Yes," Steven said. "When we couldn't find Geoffrey and we found we'd missed the bus, we asked a policeman if he had seen him—and then later on the same policeman called us, and said you'd telephoned."

"What did you do with the time until the next bus left?" I asked.

"We went back to the ring and saw everything over again," said Victoria.

I sighed.

"And we thought you might be dead!" Helen burst out reproachfully.

Victoria hung her head and said in a very small voice, "Sorry…"

"Well—did you enjoy it, apart from getting lost?" I asked her.

"Oh, *yes*," said Victoria, looking up with shining eyes. "The horses were lovely—in the musical ride they trotted and cantered to music. And we saw the jumping, and one of the horses put its feet down in front of the jump and slipped, and the rider came off over its head, and landed hanging by one leg on top of the gate!"

"And there was a Scots band playing the bagpipes, and they did a sword dance," said Steven.

"And one of the Scotsmen pulled my hair," said Victoria, blushing.

"Can we have something to eat?" asked Steven. "I'm awfully hungry."

"Help us get a meal, then," I said; and we set about preparing a very late supper.

The meal took a long time, because the children were all talking at once, and it was midnight before we got to bed. I tucked them all in, and went into my bedroom with a lighted candle, quietly so as not to wake Carol, who was asleep in her cot.

As I closed the door, a black fluttering thing flicked in through the open window and nearly into my face, and continued gyrating erratically and soundlessly round my head.

I nearly screamed. Then, feeling I had had enough for one day, I went and called the boys.

"Steven, Geoffrey! Could you come and help if you're still awake? There's a bat in my room!"

Steven and Geoffrey got up sleepily and went back with me. The bat was still flying wildly round and round the room.

"I don't know how to get it out," I said wearily.

"We shall never catch it," said Geoffrey. "They're equipped with radar."

"Can't we flick it down with something?" said Steven. "And then put it out of the window?"

"We can try," I said. "I don't want it to get into Carol's cot."

We armed ourselves with towels and nappies and started flicking. The bat flew round and round, and before long our heads kept turning automatically round and round trying to follow it. Every time we flicked, the bat wasn't there. After a time it made me feel dizzy.

"If only it would keep *still!*" complained Steven.

Carol sat up in her cot, looked at us in amazement, and laughed. It became increasingly like a nightmare. Geoffrey flicked, Steven flicked, I flicked, and the bat flew round and round and round and round… It must have looked like some weird primitive ceremonial dance. The candle flame flickered, and Carol clapped her hands and bounced up and down with delight.

"It would happen tonight!" groaned Geoffrey, aiming another ineffectual flick with his towel.

"I can't go to bed with it in the room," I pleaded. "And it might land on Carol."

Steven launched a mighty sweep with a blanket, missed the bat, and hit the candle—putting it out. We were left in darkness, while the fluttering of the bat's wings swept over our heads.

"Get a light, quickly!" I cried, and we all collided in the middle of the room as we hunted for the matches. I found them on the floor, and in a few seconds got the candle alight again.

And the bat had gone.

We stood looking round the room unbelievingly, wondering if we'd dreamed it.

"It must have been the light that attracted it in," said Geoffrey. "As soon as the candle went out, the sky outside looked lighter than the room, so it flew out of the window."

"Why didn't we think of that before?" said Steven.

"Well—you did it!" I said.

"Just what I thought when you didn't turn up at the bus stop," grumbled Geoffrey, as they both went back to bed. "*Bats*!"

21

Condemned Property

As time went on, it became apparent that it would be no use cleaning the house thoroughly again until the ceiling was repaired in the weenybedes' room. Dust and dirt from inside the roof fell continuously through the rafters and spread through the house. No amount of brushing could get the dirt out of the carpets, and did in fact only make more dust everywhere else. I soon realized that we should have to take the carpets up altogether—and burn them, probably, as they were not worth having cleaned, and the dust had sunk too deeply into the pile to beat or even wash out.

"Shall we get new carpets, then?" asked Helen.

"Or linoleum," I said. "It would be easier to keep clean—I think it was a mistake to put down carpets, with so much mud all round us, in the first place."

But it was also obvious that there was no point in putting down anything new until we had got rid of the flow of dust and dirt from the roof. And if we had the ceiling put up, we ought to have the walls repaired at the same time; we could not upheave the whole household twice. And then there were the windows and the door latches and the bathroom wall and the back door... and all the other things—and the expense, as well as the disorganization it would involve, would mount up. I began to wonder whether the house was worth spending any more on; and if not, what was the alternative, as we could not live indefinitely in its present state of disintegration.

"Why does everything always happen at once?" I complained to Geoffrey. "When something goes wrong, everything else does too..."

"Perhaps you only notice other things more, when something bigger happens," said Geoffrey. "It makes you start worrying about other things that were really there all the time."

"Yes, but they do all seem to have got worse suddenly," I said. "Perhaps it's just the effect of the damp and all that bad weather on an old house—plus occupation by a large and energetic family…"

Whatever it was, the house seemed to be falling to pieces round us, and the more I thought about it, the more I didn't know where to start.

While I was thinking, we cleaned up the house as best we could and tacked up sheets of paper over Nicholas's cot, so the dust would not fall on his face while he slept. As the weather grew steadily warmer, it didn't matter so much about the weenybedes' unintended skylight; in fact, as Victoria had said, they rather liked lying in bed and watching the birds flying past over their heads. And I felt that in the middle of the summer it might be easier to cope with the complications of builders and babies in a confined space, since the babies and some of the furniture could be kept out in the garden, during the day at least.

"Although what happens if they don't finish the ceiling in one day I can't think," I said. "There's nowhere to put the furniture from the weenybedes' room except piled up in our bedrooms and on the landing, and we must keep the landing clear if the men are to get up and down, and then the weenybedes won't have anywhere to sleep, as there isn't room anywhere else to put the bed and cot up; and with everything piled in our rooms we shan't be able to go to bed either."

"What we need," said Geoffrey thoughtfully, "is a new house."

This had occurred to me too. But even if we could afford it—which we couldn't—none of us wanted to leave our hill.

So we left the position as it was for a time, hoping that perhaps a solution would become apparent; and our lives resumed their normal course.

The weenybedes went on growing, and Carol got on to her feet, and suddenly we seemed to have a lot more children than before—and a lot less of everything else, including space.

The weather continued to be hot, and our pump, which had

been functioning uneventfully since the pipes to the well had been lengthened, grew more and more difficult to work; or rather, we got less and less water up for the same amount of pumping the handle. I wrote to the local Council asking if anything could be done about the water supply; and after a few days received a reply saying that my letter was receiving attention. Meanwhile, pumping became steadily more difficult.

One morning after we had finished the washing and Steven and I were preparing lunch, Steven went to get a saucepan of water for the potatoes, and there seemed to be hardly any water coming up at all.

"I'm getting about a tablespoonful per pump," complained Steven, as he put the saucepan on the stove. "And what there is, is muddy."

"That means we're nearly down to the bottom of the well," said Geoffrey cheerfully.

"I know," I said. "And when they lengthened the pipes they said they couldn't extend them any further, or we should draw up mud. I'll have to write to the Council again and see if anything can be done. Anyway, it's always worse after we've drawn on it for the washing. It seems to run in again after it's stood for a few hours."

"If we aren't being flooded out or snowed up, we're marooned without water," commented Geoffrey. "It makes life more interesting, of course!"

"I don't know what happens to our spoons," grumbled Steven from the kitchen, trying to find one in the appropriate drawer.

"There's one behind the settee in the sitting-room," I said, "and three in the playroom—and I saw two out in the garden yesterday, and I think there's one on top of the rabbit hutch in the shed…"

"How do they get *there*?" demanded Steven crossly.

Victoria and Helen looked guilty.

"The weenybedes love playing with them," said Victoria. "And Carol likes biting on them now she's getting her back teeth through."

"Does Anna like playing with them too?" asked Geoffrey.

"No—Christopher took that one out," said Helen. "He and Nicholas were playing mud-pies."

"You mustn't take things out of the kitchen drawers," Steven reproved Christopher. "You don't need spoons to make mud pies."

"Yes, me does," said Christopher imperturbably.

"Well, I can't make sauce without a spoon," said Steven. "Can't you give them something else to play with, Victoria? Babies don't have to have spoons!"

"You all did," I said reflectively, as Victoria retrieved the missing ones and took them through into the kitchen. "I always used to wonder what the attraction was when you were little. I remember once I bought a set of six silver teaspoons, and you took them all out and dropped them into a big oil can in the garden. We never did find all of them again..."

"They were these ones, weren't they?" asked Victoria, holding up a battered silver spoon.

"Yes, that's right," I said. "That's the only one we've got left."

"Well, what about *knives*?" demanded Steven. "I only want to cut a piece of butter, and there's not a single knife in the drawer..."

"Oh, Christopher had one to cut a piece of string in the garden," said Helen. "I'll go and fetch it..."

"I think the others are in the other drawer," I said pacifically, as Steven showed signs of exploding.

"It would be easier if the weenybedes had a proper playroom," said Victoria. "They're getting too old now to stay in the pantry."

There was a sudden shout from Geoffrey, engrossed in books in the sitting-room.

"Can't someone look after Nicholas? He's pottering about with his pot!"

"Very appropriate," I said, rescuing the pot and replacing it firmly under its owner. "There was nothing in it, anyway."

"There never is," said Helen sadly.

Nicholas was a problem over potting. Not that he minded sitting on it—in that respect he was most co-operative—but he never by any chance *used* it. We had given up hope of having him trained quickly, and were thankful that at least he had no objection to trying; and only restricted him when, in moments of exuberance, he got up and threw his pot up in the air—because, after all, it might have something in it one day.

"Never mind," I said now. "He'll come to it in time. You needn't complain, Geoffrey, you were just as difficult!"

Nicholas sat placidly on his pot in the middle of the floor. "Doo wun," he said.

"Well, *do* do one!" said Geoffrey, returning to his studies.

Helen gazed pensively out of the window.

"What are you thinking about, Helen?" I asked her.

She turned dreamy eyes into the room.

"Lots of things," she said. "I can't think of all the things I think!"

"Can you think of any of them?" Steven teased her. Helen threw a cushion at him.

"Can we have the wireless on?" asked Victoria. She went over to it and twiddled the knobs. A raucous jazz band filled the room.

"Oh, turn it off!" said Geoffrey crossly.

"I'll see if I can get some music," said Victoria.

"What do you call that, then?" asked Helen.

Victoria looked surprised. "Jazz isn't meant to be musical, is it?" she said.

"It's meant to be, but it isn't," said Steven.

Geoffrey looked up again.

"Have you seen the notices about the new television service?" he asked. He took a leaflet out of his pocket, showing on the cover a magnified view of a man's eye looking down the sights of a gun.

"What does it say about it?" asked Steven.

Geoffrey turned to the inside of the leaflet. More pictures showed a selection of future programmes.

"Well, there's another picture of a man with a gun," he said, "and then a picture of two men with guns—and then one of two policemen with revolvers…"

"How nice," I said. "Anything else?"

"Then there's a picture of a scene in hospital," said Geoffrey.

"Quite naturally," I said. "There's one comfort about living up here—we *can't* have television!"

There was a knock at the back door, and Steven opened it. Outside our garden gate stood a shiny black car, and on the doorstep stood a man in a shiny black suit.

"Good morning," he said. "I've come about the water."

"Why, do you want some?" I asked, taken by surprise. We were used to men coming from the fields and asking for water, either to drink or for the stock, but this man seemed unlikely to need either.

"Only a sample," he replied. "I'm from the Public Health department of the Council. You wrote to us about your difficulty with the well. I've come to look at the pump and take a sample of the water for testing. We have had a number of cases of water becoming polluted in these shallow wells during the dry weather, so it's as well to be on the safe side."

"Yes, of course," I said. "Come in. I was going to write to you again as I hadn't heard—the well seems to be practically dry now, and there's mud coming up with the water."

He clicked his tongue. "That's bad," he said, and followed me into the kitchen.

I showed him the pump, and he produced what looked like a small blow-lamp, and proceeded to apply the flame to the spout, interestedly watched by the children. "We have to sterilize it," he explained. "There might be local contamination on the spout, not present in the water." He tried the handle. "It's certainly low," he agreed.

Laboriously he pumped a container full of water, and poured it into a small bottle, on which he stuck a label bearing the words, "Sample produced by..." and wrote in my name, which struck me as being slightly inaccurate. Noting the direction of my eyes, he explained hastily that the labels he was using were really meant for samples of milk from dairy farms...

"We shall let you know about that in a few days' time," he said. "Now about your present water supply—we can have water delivered to you until the well fills up again. We do deliver regularly to a number of houses round here which have unsuitable or inadequate wells. We can put up a tank in your garden, holding about a hundred and fifty gallons, and fill it as required. It has to be paid for, of course," he added. "It works out at about twelve or fifteen shillings per delivery."

I did rapid mental arithmetic. For the amount of water we normally used, that would amount to more than the rent of the house...

I sighed.

"You'd better do that then—thank you," I said.

He collected his things and went to the door, nearly tripping over Carol, who had escaped from the playroom and come through to see what was happening on the way.

"We'll have the water delivered to you first thing tomorrow morning," he said; and a few minutes later we heard the car bumping down the field again.

The next day a lorry arrived outside our gate, much to the delight of Christopher and Nicholas, and unloaded a large water tank with a tap at the bottom, which they installed in our garden and filled with water from a tank mounted on the lorry. This certainly made life much easier, and for the first time for nearly three years we were able to get water from a tap; but I couldn't help thinking about the cost if the drought went on for very long, and wishing for once that it would rain.

Several days later the shiny black car drove up the field again, and the first man came to the door accompanied by another in a brown tweed suit.

"I'm afraid we have bad news for you," said the brown tweed one, when I opened the door. "Do you normally drink the water from this well?"

I said we did.

"Well, don't," he said. The sample we took showed a serious degree of contamination—" he went on into technical details which were beyond me.

"But it was tested before we moved in," I protested. "And I was told that it was reasonably pure, but it would be advisable to boil or filter drinking water—and we always have. And people have been drinking it, unboiled, for hundreds of years, and—except for the man who they say hanged himself in the barn—they all died of old age. Do you mean the water isn't safe now?"

"Well, we wouldn't say that exactly," he replied. "As you say, people have been drinking it for many years. But it is probable that you have used considerably more water than most previous residents here—" he glanced out at our three lines full of washing—"and that, coupled with the exceptionally dry season, has caused the water to sink to a very low level. Certainly the water you are now getting up from that well is not fit to drink. There have," he added severely, "been a number of cases of typhoid in this area recently, traced to the wells. And if anything like that were discovered in this water, the property would of course have to be condemned."

"You mean we couldn't live here?" I asked, not quite taking it in.

"You would be ordered to leave," he responded firmly.

"But at present we can stay provided we don't drink the water? Does that mean we shall have to have water delivered all the time from now on?"

"You will have to have it delivered for drinking purposes, yes," he agreed. "You can of course use the pump water, when the well fills up, for washing and so on. But on the other hand, it is not advisable to have the water standing in the tank for too long. It should be used and refilled often enough to prevent its becoming stale." He looked at the pump. "The sample we took was definitely very unsatisfactory," he said. "You have a large family here, and I should definitely advise you to start looking for other accommodation. We can supply you with water during the summer but—" he paused and looked out of the open door, "—*not* during wet weather. It would be quite impossible to get the water-carrier up the field."

Stunned, I watched them preparing to go.

"They're very odd things, wells," he said. "No accounting for what you'll find. Your well here—that's never been much good. But only a few hundred yards from here, the well up at those old cottages—" he pointed up the loke, "—perfectly pure water— always has been. It's a pity, but there it is." They walked through the doorway, and the first man turned and said, "Let us know when you need more water, and we'll have it brought up."

Then they had gone—leaving us with a new and bigger problem than all the ones that had gone before.

Slowly I went back into the sitting-room, where the children were waiting, gazing towards the kitchen with consternation in their faces.

"Did you hear all that?" I asked them. "We're condemned!"

"Not quite, are we," Geoffrey demurred.

"No, but as good as," I pointed out. "You do all feel all right, do you?" I added anxiously. "Apparently we've been drinking contaminated water all this time."

"But we boiled it," said Steven. "It should be all right boiled, shouldn't it?"

"Apparently not, now," I said.

"Perhaps it is because of the dry weather," said Geoffrey. "We're getting water from right at the bottom of the well now..."

"And stirring up things in the mud," I said. "Anyway, we've got a supply of pure water now in the tank. But it looks as if we shall have to move before the winter, though I don't know where to, because in wet weather they won't be able to get the water lorry up the field. And the annoying thing is that he says the water in the well up at the cottages is absolutely pure..."

I broke off, struck by a sudden thought.

"The cottages!" I exclaimed. "We could move into the cottages!"

"We couldn't!" said Steven. "There aren't any windows or floors!"

"But suppose we could buy them?" I persisted. "They can't be worth much as they are. But if we could have them put in order—we could have the work done bit by bit, as we could afford it—instead of paying for repairs here. And once we'd bought them and got the well put in order, we could fetch drinking water from there—all through the winter. It wouldn't matter then how long it took before they were ready to live in—we could stay here until they were."

"The two of them would be bigger than this house," said Geoffrey. "We should have more space."

"We should be able to stay on our hill," said Victoria.

"And we could move everything out of the garden, quite easily," said Steven.

"We'll make inquiries, anyway," I said.

"When?" demanded Helen.

"Now!" said Geoffrey and Steven and Victoria and I together.

22

Their Flocks by Night

If our first autumn at the House on the Hill had been the wettest for many years, this summer was the hottest in living memory. We had no more trouble with mud in the house—the track up our field was as hard as the concrete path; our flowers drooped in earth as dry as dust; our well went dry altogether, so we were entirely dependent on the weekly supply from the Council; and the pond at the back of the house grew smaller and smaller, the water retreating before an ever-widening stretch of slowly drying mud.

I took Helen for her day at the sea; and then we took the weenybedes for a day as well. The sun shone out of a cloudless blue sky, and it was so hot that even the sea was like a warm bath. Christopher and Nicholas played in the warm pools, and made sand castles in the warm damp sand; and Carol ran about the beach delightedly, although rather surprised at first by the feel of sand between her toes.

There were no cattle on the fields round us now, only the three horses—there wasn't enough grass; but late in the summer, our landlord brought a flock of white-faced sheep from the farm and put them on the big field behind the house.

"But how he thinks they're going to get water, I don't know," said Geoffrey. "The grass is all dried up, and there's practically no water left in the pond—and what there is they can't reach for the mud."

"The horses have to wade right in up to their knees," said Victoria. "But it's all right for them, they're tall enough to do it, and they like water muddy anyway."

One evening, just as it was starting to get dusk, Steven was out getting hogweed for the rabbits and Helen and Victoria and I were starting to get the weenybedes' bath ready when Geoffrey came in, and said quietly, "There's a sheep stuck in the mud in the pond. I'm afraid it will go under if we leave it. Can someone come and help me get it out?"

"You go, Victoria," I said.

After she and Geoffrey had gone I said to Helen, "I'd better go and see if they need help. Keep the weenybedes happy and look after Carol," and I put on boots and went out to the pond.

The sheep was in the mud up to its neck, with only its back and head showing. Geoffrey had already waded in nearly up to his knees, and was standing by the sheep's head with his arms under its fore-quarters, heaving with all his strength; while Victoria had fetched a plank and was laying it across the mud between him and the bank.

"I can't move her—she's stuck fast," Geoffrey said. "See if you can get hold of her hind-quarters, Victoria."

Victoria walked out along the plank to the rear end of the sheep. They both heaved together, and there was a squelching sound as they raised the sheep a few inches, but she slipped back again.

"Geoffrey, be careful," I said. "How deep is it?"

"I'm standing on the bottom now," said Geoffrey. "And I think she is too, but she's held in too tightly by the mud to pull herself out. I'll try to pull her front feet round onto the plank."

Again they both heaved, and again the mud gave, and the sheep emerged for a few seconds—and then slipped back again.

"There's nothing to get a grip of," said Victoria, "except wool, and we don't want to pull it off."

"Would the spade help—or a rope?" I asked.

"Yes, if you can find one," said Geoffrey.

"There's a rope somewhere in the shed that Helen and I had playing horses," said Victoria.

"All right, I'll go and get it," I said.

"Bring the spade too," called Geoffrey.

I climbed over the gate again and ran back to the house. The spade was standing by the back door, but I couldn't find the rope. I looked into the sitting-room and found Helen playing trains with all three weenybedes. It was getting darker every minute now. I took the spade and ran back to the pond.

Walking out along the plank, I handed the spade to Geoffrey. He took it and dug it in under the sheep.

"That's better—she's got her front feet on it," he said. "If I heave her up, can you pull her over, Victoria, onto the plank?"

Again they both heaved, Victoria balanced precariously on the plank, while I stood on the other end to keep it steady. Suddenly the mud gave, and the sheep's front feet emerged, struggling to get a grip. Slowly they pulled her round, but her feet slithered off the plank and she slipped back into the mud; but now her head was facing towards the bank.

"She's nearly there now," I said. "If you get back here, Geoffrey, we should be able to pull her out."

"I can't!" cried Geoffrey. "I can't move!" He struggled to lift his feet. "My legs are stuck!"

"Don't panic!" I said. "Can you pull your feet out of your boots?"

"I think so." He tried cautiously. "But I can't leave my boots in the pond!"

"You'll have to," I said. "Better than leaving *you* in the pond. And we can't get the sheep out without you. Step out on to the plank—we'll try to rescue your boots afterwards."

Leaning on the spade, Geoffrey withdrew first one foot and then the other and, leaving his boots sticking up out of the mud, stepped on to the plank in his bare feet. Victoria stayed on the other end of the plank to keep it steady. The sheep watched us with calm eyes in which were both resignation and despair.

"Lucky she's got the sense not to struggle when it's no use," said Geoffrey.

"It's a pity *she* isn't wearing boots!" said Victoria.

Geoffrey took a deep breath and bent down to take hold of the sheep again, with Victoria on the other side.

"Couldn't we get another plank to put in front of her?" I said.

"There is another one by the gate," said Victoria.

It was now getting too dark to see clearly, and I couldn't find the plank, but I stumbled over a small sheet of corrugated iron by the barn, and brought it back to the pond.

"Put it down as close to her as you can," said Geoffrey. "Now, when we lift her, try to push it under her feet…" He and Victoria heaved at the sheep's neck. Her feet emerged, kicking wildly, and I pushed the metal sheet under them. She got a grip on it and, with Geoffrey and Victoria pushing behind, heaved her hind-quarters out, staggered forward, and fell on her side on the dried mud of the bank.

"We've done it!" cried Geoffrey.

"Is she all right?" asked Victoria anxiously.

"I think she's just collapsed from exhaustion," I said.

We looked at the sheep uncertainly. She lay very still in the half-light. Geoffrey went down on his knees and put his head against her side.

"Her heart's beating," he said.

"Shall I get her some water?" suggested Victoria. "It's what she went into the pond for in the first place."

"Good idea," said Geoffrey, and Victoria ran off into the darkness.

She came back with a shallow dish full of water, which I took from her over the gate, and we held it to the sheep's nose. She didn't drink any, but the smell seemed to revive her. With a bound she sprang up, and then stood there, trembling, at the edge of the pond.

"For heaven's sake don't let her get back into it," said Geoffrey, moving cautiously behind her.

"We'd better drive her down to the bottom of the field, with the others," said Victoria. "Then perhaps she won't come back here and get stuck again."

"I think we ought to bring them some water," said Geoffrey. "They'll all keep getting into the pond if we don't."

"First we'd better rescue your boots," I said. "If we leave them any longer they may sink over the tops and out of sight."

Gently we drove the sheep down the field, until we saw her join the rest of the flock. Then we returned to the pond and surveyed the boots. Only the tops were visible now, and when Geoffrey walked out along the plank and tugged at them he found they were up to the rims in the mud.

"I can't move them—I can't even get a grip," he said.

"Couldn't we thread a bit of string through the holes in the tops," I suggested. "That would give you a handle to pull on."

Geoffrey stood up and felt through his pockets, and finally produced a ragged piece of string. He bent down again and felt round the boots.

After a time he said crossly, "It's no good! It won't go through!"

"Shall I try?" I asked. "I'm quite good at threading needles in the dark."

Geoffrey came back and I cautiously walked out along the plank, while he and Victoria stood on the other end. Crouched on the plank I felt very insecure, but I groped for the boots, found a hole, and started manipulating the string.

"Be careful you don't fall in!" called Geoffrey anxiously.

After several tries I got the string through the first boot, knotted it into a loop—and pulled. The mud heaved, the boot jerked up—and the string broke. But I grabbed the top of the boot and pulled it free.

"That's one, anyway!" I called to Geoffrey. "Have you got any more string?"

"No—but let me try to get the other one," said Geoffrey.

We changed places, and as I reached dry land again Steven appeared out of the darkness and joined us on the bank.

"Helen said you were down here rescuing a sheep," he said. "Is it out yet?"

"The sheep's out," I said. "We're just rescuing Geoffrey's boots."

"Why, did he lose them?" asked Steven.

"He didn't lose them exactly," I said. "He got stuck in the mud too, and had to step out of them to get out.—Is it coming?" I asked Geoffrey.

"Not yet," said Geoffrey, tugging hard.

"Can I help?" asked Steven.

"You could come out here and get the spade under it," said Geoffrey.

So Steven walked out along the plank, and peered down into the black mud for the boot.

"I can't even see it!" he said.

"Here, by my hand," explained Geoffrey.

Steven dug the spade in and heaved. Geoffrey pulled, there was a squelch and a plop, and they both nearly toppled backwards into the mud.

"Got it!" called Geoffrey triumphantly, and they felt their way precariously back to the bank.

It was now nearly dark, and stars were appearing in the sky overhead.

"We'd better take the sheep some water before it gets any darker," said Geoffrey, putting on his boots again and trying to brush some of the mud off his arms.

"You and Steven do that," I said. "Victoria and I had better go in and see to the weenybedes."

When we reached the house we found Helen sitting on the settee with Carol in her arms, and Christopher and Nicholas one each side of her, fast asleep.

"Have you got the sheep out?" asked Helen.

"Yes—and the boys are taking them some water now," I said. "You can go and help if you like."

Helen ran out, and Victoria and I bathed the weenybedes quickly and got them to bed.

When they were safely tucked in we went out again and met Geoffrey and Steven and Helen coming back with empty buckets. It was quite dark now and the sky was full of stars.

"We've filled the metal feeding trough with water," said Geoffrey. "They were terribly thirsty, but they've all had a drink now, and they should be all right for tonight."

He pushed his hair back wearily with a muddy hand. "You don't think I ought to stay up and watch them in case any of them get in again, do you?"

"No, I think they'll be all right now," I said. "And my bedroom window looks over the pond—I should hear if one did get stuck again. Is our sheep all right?"

"Yes, she came up for water with the others," said Geoffrey.

Behind us came the occasional peaceful bleating of the flock. I looked up at the sky, and saw the Plough shining brilliantly over our heads.

"One day, Geoffrey," I said, "we'll get you a farm."

23

Venture into Space

Having accepted the idea that a move, eventually, was inevitable, other things that had been worrying me began to fall into place, and our plans for the immediate future started to take shape. We then began to find snags.

The first thing we had to do was to find out if it would be possible to buy the cottages, at a price that would be within our range; and then to get a builder to look over them and report on the prospects of putting them into repair.

The owner of the cottages was willing to sell very reasonably—*but* there was an additional field, besides the half-acre on which the cottages stood, which he wanted to sell with them; pointing out, quite rightly, that this field, sandwiched between the cottages and the cornfields up the loke, would be virtually useless on its own to anyone else. It was only two acres, but it was more land than we needed; and unless we could do something with it, more than we could afford.

But Geoffrey was enthusiastic. "We could keep chickens—and a cow," he said. "I could milk it—and we could sell any surplus eggs, as well as supplying all the eggs and milk we should need ourselves."

"And we could keep Snowy on the field," said Victoria wistfully. Her acquisition of the pony, promised a year ago, had been further delayed owing to the difficulty of finding anywhere to keep him; for, as Victoria said, if he stayed on our landlord's fields, he wouldn't really feel like *her* horse.

"We could have all the half-acre round the cottages for a garden," said Steven hopefully. "We could grow our own vegetables, as well as flowers."

"It would be lovely to have a field of our own," sighed Helen.

So we had almost made up our minds about that, when we encountered the second snag—the builder's report.

I was out when the builder called, and he inspected the cottages in my absence; but he left a depressing little note stating simply that they were "beyond repair."

Further inquiries, however, established that the outer walls and foundations were still sound, and some parts of the roof; but the entire interior was falling to pieces, and would have to be pulled out and re-built, which in view of the isolated position of the place, the builder for his part regarded as being a waste of time.

But we didn't agree.

"It means we'd just have the shell of a house, to start with," I said thoughtfully. "But after all, isn't that what we want? We can have the interior stripped, and the roof and windows mended, and the well put in order, straight away. And then we can arrange the inside to suit our needs, in our own time."

"We can start using the land straight away, too," Geoffrey said.

"And get Snowy," said Victoria.

"And we could start making the garden," said Steven. "We could get the land cleared, and dig out paths."

"There's a lot of undergrowth we'll have to cut down," said Geoffrey. "There are brambles and nettles right up to the doors."

"Can I help the builders?" asked Helen.

"We'd better go and have a look," I said, "and see what will have to be done."

So Geoffrey, Steven, Helen and I went up to the cottages with a tape measure, and pushed our way through the brambles—"It's like the Sleeping Beauty's palace!" said Helen—and measured up the space inside, Geoffrey crawling through a hole in the ceiling, which had once been a staircase, to get at the bedrooms above.

Trails of ivy grew through the broken window frames; there was a huge pile of twigs and dried grass in one corner, which Geoffrey informed us was an accumulation of birds' nests, used and abandoned over the years the cottages had stood empty. Outside the windows, laden fruit trees stood knee-deep in the long grass, and even in their present state the four walls had the feeling of a home, only waiting, like the Sleeping Beauty's palace, for someone to care enough to break through the brambles and bring it to life again.

I looked at it all, and decided that we had found our new home.

When we had sorted out the measurements, we found we could have, downstairs, a kitchen-dining-room, with adjoining scullery, a hall, with a cupboard for coats and boots, a sitting-room, and a bathroom; and upstairs, five bedrooms, three large and two small. If we wanted an extra playroom we would have to build it on, but the space for building was there.

"It's just right," said Victoria.

"And *we* shall be our nearest neighbours now!" said Helen.

The next thing that became apparent was that although, if we were not staying permanently at the House on the Hill, it was not worthwhile having any major repairs done—in fact, we couldn't, as all our resources would have to go into the new house—we must still do something to deal with the worst dilapidations, and particularly the weenybedes' ceiling.

So Geoffrey went in to our ironmonger's and made inquiries, and came back with full instructions on how to put up ceiling boards. A few days later, five large boards, a box of nails, a roll of paper tape, and a packet of powdered glue were delivered to the bottom of our drift.

Geoffrey and Steven brought them up the field, and, the next day, took them upstairs immediately after breakfast and started work. We stripped everything out of the weenybedes' room again—for the fourth time that year—and I left Geoffrey sorting out boards and instructions, until he called plaintively down the stairs for someone to help, because he found he couldn't hold the boards up with his head while using both hands to hammer in the nails.

Steven, Victoria and Helen took it in turns to go and hold up the boards for him; and gradually the ceiling took shape, despite a good many slips, and nails dropped down the others' necks.

By the end of the day, Geoffrey had nailed all the boards into position, stuffed newspaper round the edges, and pasted the tape over the joins. The result, if not professional-looking, was at least adequate. What was more, when Steven and Helen had washed out the room again, it smelled clean and fresh, and no more dust fell down to spread over everything. We got the furniture back just in time before the weenybedes went to bed, and Christopher and Nicholas lay looking up in wonderment at their third change of ceiling that year.

This done, we set about really cleaning the house. We took up the stair and landing carpets, and washed the boards; and I bought yards of inexpensive linoleum, mostly in remnants at the sales, to put down instead. Steven and I struggled with the laying of it, finding that half-unrolled linoleum seems to have a life and a will of its own—but eventually getting disentangled from it, cutting it into shape, and tacking it firmly into place. We cut strips of linoleum to put on the stairs, which took longer than we had anticipated, since we soon found out that no two stairs were the same size or shape, so each one had to be measured separately and the linoleum carefully cut to fit.

We laid new linoleum all through the house, after we had got rid of the dust and dirt. We patched up the windows, and resigned ourselves to temporary door-latches; and as the summer drew to a close, we prepared to deal with another winter at the House on the Hill.

With the coming of autumn, the children began to look forward to fireworks night; and now Christopher and Nicholas were old enough to join in too.

The Fifth was a clear, brilliant night, with not too bright a moon but a lot of stars, and after a late tea we put Carol to bed, and we all wrapped up in warm clothes while I got out the box of fireworks and several boxes of matches, and assembled in the kitchen ready to start.

"Make sure all the cats are indoors first," I said. "Christopher, open the door and let that cat through."

"Oh, me *keeps* opening doors!" said Christopher, impatient with excitement. "Oh, all right, cat…!" And eventually we got them all through into the sitting-room and shut the door.

"I've got everything ready outside," said Geoffrey. "A bottle for the rockets, and a jam-jar for the small ones, and a box of damp earth…"

"Have you got pins for the pin-wheels?" asked Steven.

"I've got those," I said. "Look, catch Nicholas!" He had climbed up on to a chair to look into the box of fireworks, and the chair was slipping. Helen made a dive for him too late, and he rolled on to the floor, not sure whether to laugh or cry.

"Are you did fall down?" inquired Christopher anxiously, running over to comfort him.

"I can't find Christopher's boots!" called Victoria from the bathroom.

But eventually we got everything and everyone in order, and we all went outside.

I put the box of fireworks down by the hedge, and Geoffrey and I started letting them off. Rockets soared over the house, roman candles and fountains sent stars and sprays of colour into the still air, and one described as a "flying saucer" whizzed away nearly into the boys' bedroom window. Christopher and Nicholas held tightly on to Victoria and Helen, and squeaked every time one went off.

In all the excitement I had forgotten to cover the box of fireworks. I lit a roman candle, and cascades of stars flew into the air. And one of them landed in the open box.

Suddenly there was a hissing and popping, and fireworks started flying in all directions. Rockets sped horizontally along the ground, leaving a trail of coloured stars, pin-wheels whirled in the grass, and a sizzling mass of colour lit up the garden.

The children scattered, half frightened, half excited, while for a few seconds we watched the most effective set-piece I had ever managed to provide. Only I didn't really have a chance to appreciate it—I was being chased across the garden by one of the biggest rockets…

It was all over in a minute and in the silence that followed Steven inquired, "Why didn't you tell us you were going to do that?"

Returning breathless, after outwitting the rocket at the last moment, I explained that I didn't know I was.

After that we went indoors and had hot chocolate, and we turned the lights out while Christopher held a sparkler all by himself. It took quite a long time to get the weenybedes to bed, but at last Nicholas was in his cot, calling out to us all, "Awa! Awa! Happy deem!"—and Christopher was in his pyjamas ready to go up when he turned to me pleadingly.

"Can we have more morning-night?" (morning-night meant tomorrow) he asked...

"More what?" asked Geoffrey.

Christopher took a deep breath, not being sure of the word "fireworks."

"You know—stick it in mud, match the top, ssss!—up in the air!" he explained. "More *that*!"

24

Highland Fling

As soon as it was settled that we should buy the cottages, we arranged with the owner to let us have the well repaired, and take drinking water from it; and by then winter had come. The grass in the fields was white with frost, and our washing hung stiff on the lines outside.

Christopher, Nicholas, and Carol played happily in the sitting-room, and climbed in and out of the playpen; and our current crop of four kittens climbed up the furniture and sat on our shoulders, and sometimes even on the top of my head during meals.

One morning in December, I came downstairs as usual, lit the fire in the sitting-room, put the kettle on for tea, put the milk and water on in the big double saucepan for porridge, went up and put Christopher and Nicholas on their pots, and called the others. Then I came down again, made the tea, and lifted the lid of the porridge saucepan to see if the milk was ready to put the porridge in.

And the saucepan blew up.

There was a loud explosion, the top part of the saucepan was flung out—fortunately I kept hold of the handle, so only a little of the milk was spilt—and all the boiling water in the bottom part was thrown over my arms.

I called frantically to Geoffrey, and plunged my arms into a bowl of cold water that we kept standing by the sink to use if we needed to prime the pump.

Geoffrey came running downstairs.

"What's happened?" he asked, staring in astonishment at my

dripping wet arms, and the steaming water splashed all over the kitchen floor.

"The porridge saucepan blew up," I explained, pulling off my cardigan. My arms were red and burning from wrist to elbow.

"Blew up? How?" demanded Geoffrey.

"I don't know," I said. I went through into the sitting-room and shakily sat down. "I just lifted the lid, and—it did blow up."

Geoffrey examined the saucepan interestedly.

"The top part must have got stuck in the bottom part," he said. "So the steam couldn't escape, and built up pressure inside—and when you lifted the lid, it all forced its way out. It's lucky it missed your face."

"Put it back on again, if you think it will be all right," I said. "But you can make the porridge—and get me something to put over my arms."

Geoffrey refilled the bottom part of the saucepan with water and put the whole thing back onto the stove.

"I'll make sure it doesn't get stuck again," he said. "What shall I get for you?"

"Two big handkerchiefs to cover the burns," I told him. "And I think you'd better go to the doctor for a dressing and a sedative—it's hurting rather a lot."

Geoffrey fetched the handkerchiefs, and helped me to tie them loosely over the scalded places.

"The doctor's surgery will be open in about twenty minutes," he said. "If I go now I should be able to see him without waiting. I'll call Steven to look after the porridge."

Steven came down as Geoffrey got his coat on.

"What's happened?" he wanted to know.

"The porridge saucepan blew up," I explained. "No, I don't know how," I added quickly, anticipating the next question. "It wasn't anything I did. Ask Geoffrey."

"The steam got trapped in the bottom part," Geoffrey enlightened him. "And the pressure blew the boiling water out..."

"But why did it?" asked Steven. "And is it going to do it again...?" He approached the saucepan with caution.

"I shouldn't think so," I said. "We've been using that saucepan for fifteen years and it's never done it before."

"See that the top part is loose in the bottom part," advised Geoffrey. "So long as the steam keeps escaping round the middle it'll be all right.... I'll get off to the doctor," he added to me, and went out of the door.

Steven set about cautiously tending the porridge. I was beginning to feel rather odd, and my arms were throbbing with pain.

"Ask Victoria to get Carol up and give her her breakfast when she's dressed Christopher and Nicholas," I told Steven.

I went upstairs and lay down on my bed.

After a little while Victoria came in and lifted Carol out of her cot.

"Done *dee*!" announced Carol, pointing to her nappies.

"I'll change them, then," said Victoria. "What happened?" she asked me. "Are you all right?"

"The porridge saucepan blew up," I explained again, feeling that I was going to have to say this a great many times during the next few days. "The water scalded my arms—Geoffrey's gone to the doctor. I'm all right, but it was a horrible shock."

Victoria sat down on the end of my bed and started dressing Carol, who kept twisting round to look at me. She had just finished when the door opened and Helen came in.

"What's happened to you?" she asked.

"The porridge saucepan blew up," I said. "Go and help Victoria to look after the weenybedes."

When they had gone downstairs, I lay back and tried not to think about my arms.

I heard steps on the stairs and Steven came in.

"The porridge is ready," he said, "and Victoria is seeing to the weenybedes. The saucepan was all right—I let the steam out like Geoffrey said. As soon as they've finished, I'll get our breakfast."

At last I heard Geoffrey's voice downstairs, and he came in with his hands full of packages.

"I saw the doctor, and he's told me what to do," he said as he shut the door. "You take two of these tablets for the pain—Steven's bringing a glass of water—and I've got dressings for the scalds. I didn't have to wait—there was only one man waiting when I got there, and when I told him what had happened, he let me go in first—but it took some time to get the dressings ready."

He took off the handkerchiefs and spread net dressings soaked in jelly over the inflamed skin.

"Then I put this gauze over it, and then the cotton wool," he explained, "and then bandage it. Is that better?"

I lay back again with both arms neatly bandaged.

"Much more comfortable," I said thankfully. "You're a good doctor, Geoffrey."

"You'd better take the tablets now," said Geoffrey, "and then rest." He added thoughtfully, "I'd like to be a vet..."

I spent most of that day in bed, coming down in a rather dazed state for meals. In the evening, when Geoffrey rebandaged my arms, we found that they had come up in large blisters.

"The doctor said they probably would," Geoffrey reassured me. "They'll be all right, with this dressing, and you're to go and see him in three or four days."

After a few days, the blisters subsided, and when I went to see the doctor, he said the skin had grafted itself back and was healing nicely.

"But how did you *do* it?" he wanted to know.

With a resigned sigh, I explained again, "The porridge saucepan blew up..."

25

Nights of Gladness

One of the drawbacks of living in the middle of a field was the difficulty of going out after dark. In summer it made no difference—the track down the field was hard and the drift leading to the road was dry—but in winter, when the field was wet and muddy and there was a stream some six inches deep and several feet wide running across the bottom of the drift, an evening visit to the theatre involved hazards never encountered in the ordinary way.

One evening in January, I took Victoria, Helen, and Steven to the pantomime, while Geoffrey stayed at home to look after the weenybedes. We had to cycle to the village two miles away to catch the bus to the town, and it was already dark when we left.

It had been snowing heavily all day, and by then was freezing hard, with intermittent flurries of snow still coming down. Had I realized how bad the roads were, I would have left earlier and walked; but Steven and Geoffrey had cycled into the village earlier, and we arranged that Helen and Steven should leave early and walk on ahead, and Victoria and I would follow on as soon as we had settled the weenybedes in bed.

When we set off, it soon became obvious that cycling was going to be very little quicker than walking. The snow was now lying almost untouched on the road—only the tracks of one car were visible in it—and it was thick and powdery, making it increasingly hard to push the bicycles along. Repeatedly I had to get off and walk.

About halfway, we caught up with Steven and Helen. By then I had given up trying to ride—it was slower and harder than walking. I paused, breathless, and asked Steven to push my bicycle for me.

He came and took it, and we started off again. But when he tried to push the bicycle, it wouldn't move. In the few seconds that we had been standing still, the back wheel had frozen solid.

After some minutes of frantic pushing, we realized we would have to abandon it, and Steven stood it in the nearest field gateway. Victoria's lighter machine was still running, so she cycled on while Steven, Helen, and I alternately walked and ran the rest of the way to the bus. We arrived sprinkled with snow—tiaraed with diamonds as befitted a visit to the theatre—but distinctly damp and chilly when we got on the bus and it melted down the back of our necks.

When we came back five hours later, it was nearly midnight and bitterly cold. The sky was clear, and a brilliant full moon shone over the glistening frozen snow.

I told Victoria, whose bicycle was still running freely, to cycle on and see that the weenybedes were all right; and Steven, Helen, and I set off walking down the shining road.

When we reached my bicycle, Steven and I tried to take it with us, but gave up after carrying it about a hundred yards. Both wheels were frozen hard, and our fingers nearly froze too as we gripped the ice-covered metal frame. We abandoned it in another gateway, to collect when it thawed. As Steven said, it seemed improbable that anyone would steal it, unless they had brought a van for the purpose, as no one could move it until the wheels would go round.

We walked the rest of the way back and arrived almost as stiff with cold as the bicycle.

"Next time we go to the theatre," I said, "we'll wait until it's warmer."

And it did seem a good deal warmer when Victoria, Steven, and I went to the ballet one evening a month later. It had been a mild, damp day, and as we cycled down the field it started to rain.

We got down the field without difficulty and rode safely through the stream at the bottom of the drift, which was now too deep to cross on foot without rubber boots.

Halfway to the village, there was a cry from Victoria—her bicycle chain had come off. We stopped and Steven replaced the chain, but when Victoria tried to start again, the back wheel wouldn't go round. Something had got stuck, and we couldn't see what was wrong; and as it was impossible for her to ride the machine any further, we abandoned it in a ditch.

I gave Victoria my bicycle and told her to ride on with Steven and leave it for me to pick up half a mile down the road, and I followed as fast as I could on foot. When I reached my bicycle again, I remounted and rode it until I caught up with Victoria, walking on with Steven, and gave her the bicycle again; and in this way, we all reached the village—breathless, but just in time to catch the bus.

All the evening it rained steadily. We caught the last bus back again and arrived in the village just before midnight. Although the rain had stopped by then, the sky was covered with heavy clouds, and when we got off the bus it was pitch dark.

The only lights we had were on our bicycles, and being dynamo lights, they were useless unless the bicycles were moving. And with only two bicycles between the three of us, either we all had to walk, or two could cycle and leave the other one to walk alone in the dark.

We felt our way to the bicycles and set off walking together, trying to keep moving fast enough to show a gleam of light ahead.

It was difficult to make out the edge of the grass verge as we went along. On each side of the road there were deep dykes, and although we all knew the road well enough, as Steven said, things look different when it's too dark to see.

Steven walked ahead pushing his bicycle, and I followed with Victoria, pushing mine. I was concentrating on keeping my light working and keeping Steven's in view ahead, and called out every so often to Victoria by my side, whom I couldn't see.

Suddenly there was a slithering noise behind me, and when I called Victoria, there was no reply. I called again urgently, and her voice answered faintly from the side of the road.

I shouted to Steven and tried to make out where her voice was coming from. Steven came back and we felt our way towards the sound. All round us the damp darkness was like a tangible curtain that we couldn't penetrate. Then we saw a dim shape emerging out of the ditch.

Steven dropped his bicycle and helped her out. She was dazed but unhurt.

"What happened?" asked Steven.

"I just slipped in," she said. "One minute I was walking on the road, and then I felt grass under my feet and then there wasn't anything there. And I've lost my handbag."

Steven lay down on the bank of the ditch and felt round in the muddy water. More by luck than anything else he found the bag, and we emptied the water out of it and returned it to Victoria.

"Are you sure you're all right?" I asked her.

"Yes, only my feet are wet," she said.

The three of us stood in the darkness on the deserted road.

"Look," I said, "you take my bicycle, Victoria, and walk on with Steven, and I'll walk behind. Then if you do go off the road I'll see the light moving over and warn you."

So we set off again. At last we reached the bottom of our drift.

Here we were faced with another problem. It was only possible to cross the stream with dry feet on bicycles—and we were one bicycle short.

"Couldn't Victoria and I cycle over, and then I bring your bicycle back for you to get over?" suggested Steven.

"And then I'd have to bring it back for you to get over," I pointed out. "We could go on like that all night, and there'd still be one of us on the wrong side of the stream!"

"Yes, so there would," agreed Steven.

"You two cycle through it," I said. "I'll see if I can get through on foot."

The two bicycles swept through, sending up showers of spray— the stream was considerably deeper and wider than it had been when we left.

It seemed ridiculous, standing there in the middle of the night, but there was only one thing for me to do. I took my shoes off and waded through the stream in bare feet.

The water was icy cold and full of sharp stones. "If this is going to the theatre," I thought, "I'll stay at home."

I caught up with the others at the top of the drift, and we started to walk up the field. But the rain had caused our track to vanish, and we found ourselves floundering in wet, sticky mud.

"Take your shoes off," I told Victoria. "You'll only lose them in the mud, and you can always wash your feet."

I took mine off again, and we felt our way cautiously up the track. In places Victoria and I sank into the mud up to our ankles. We were thankful to reach the house and get inside.

Geoffrey and Helen looked at us in astonishment.

"Get bowls of warm water, quickly!" I told them, and we sat down and bathed our feet by the fire. Victoria was not so badly off, since she had been wearing stockings, but my feet were covered in mud up to the ankles and cut and bruised by the stones in the stream. Steven made us hot coffee and we were all glad to get to bed.

The next morning, in daylight, our night's adventures seemed remote, although we still had to rescue Victoria's bicycle from the ditch.

I went to the door to take the post in, and I thought the postman looked at me rather oddly. When I went out later in the day I realized why. Clearly marked in the mud of the field was a line of naked footprints, leading all the way up to the house.

26

Harvest Home

In January and February the weenybedes had their birthdays; and now Christopher was four, Nicholas was three, and Carol was two.

Carol had learned to climb out of her playpen, not only with the help of a chair placed near enough for her to scramble on to it, which Christopher was always ready to bring for her, but by simply throwing a leg over the top and rolling over to land on her feet on the other side.

Nicholas was a little jealous of her and needed extra cuddling to reassure him that he had not lost his place in our affections. He obviously thought that she should stay a baby and not grow up to compete with him; and every time she climbed out he ran to tell us, "Tugar *not* in playpen! Tugar not in playpen!" with great insistence until we put her back.

Helen and Victoria played horses with them, giving Christopher and Nicholas rides round the sitting-room, and Carol wanted to ride too, but she was too small to sit safely on their backs.

"Christopher could be her horse," I suggested.

"Will you give Carol a ride?" Victoria asked him.

Christopher considered for a moment, eyeing Carol thoughtfully. "Yes," he said at last, going down on hands and knees, "but she musn't make my shorts wet!"

He gave her a ride round the room, but then stood up firmly.

"Me is a farmer—*not* a horse," he explained.

"You're not a farmer yet," Steven teased him. "You're too little."

Christopher was affronted.

"What will *you* be when I'm a great big farmer?" he asked Steven, adding with scorn, "You might just be a silly beastly *man*!"

In January, Christopher and Carol both had colds, and the doctor prescribed some not-too-nasty white medicine. Carol took hers without protest, but Christopher flatly refused.

"It's quite nice, really," Victoria coaxed him. "Carol *likes* it." Christopher remained unmoved. "Carol can *have* it all, then!" he said.

Despite this, he recovered as quickly as Carol did. When the snow came, he and Nicholas were delighted, and spent the afternoon on the first day making a snowman; and at bath time, Christopher ran out and brought in a handful of snow, which he wanted to put in his bath.

At the end of February the weather was fine and warm, and there was a sunshiny emptiness about the house, as the children abandoned the sitting-room and ran out into the garden, that was to me always one of the first signs of spring.

By the time that all the negotiations over the cottages were completed, spring had come. Our daffodils were in flower again, and there were green and yellow catkins swinging in the hedges, and pale pink blossom on our almond tree.

I was alone in the house with Helen and the weenybedes when I heard that our new home was really ours at last.

"Go and call the others," I told Helen. She had always had a startlingly deep voice which she had often been told would be suitable for selling newspapers, but which was very useful for calling anyone at anything up to half a mile distant on a still day.

Helen went upstairs to the landing window and leaned out.

"*Others*!" she called, at the top of her voice.

Geoffrey, Steven, and Victoria arrived breathless to hear the news.

"We can start clearing the land now," said Geoffrey.

"And getting plans made for the re-building," I said.

"Carol will be able to have a room of her own soon," said Victoria.

"I don't really want to part with her," I sighed. Carol had never kept me awake by crying in the night, despite having got nearly all her teeth through during the past year; and sometimes I wished she would cry, just a little, to give me an excuse to pick her up and cuddle her when all the others were asleep.

"Could we have a covered drying ground?" inquired Steven, looking at the previous day's washing hanging on the indoor line, which on wet days was apt to drip down his neck at meals.

"We might," I said. "But there won't be so much washing soon—Carol will be out of nappies this year."

"Done *dee*!" Carol informed us from her playpen.

"Nicholas used his pot all day yesterday," said Victoria. "He's as good as Christopher now."

"Can I take the weenybedes up to look at the cottages?" asked Helen. "They haven't seen them yet."

"When we take the plants from the garden, shall we be able to move the Virginia creeper?" Steven asked.

"Not unless you take the bricks from the wall it's growing up, I should think," said Geoffrey. "I'd like to get a Jersey cow."

"Jersey milk for the weenybedes!" said Victoria.

"How many chickens shall we have to start with?" asked Steven.

"I don't know," I said. "We shall have to ask someone who knows about hens."

Geoffrey said tentatively, "They've got some lambs to bring up by hand at the farm. Some of them are twins, and the ewe can only feed one, and some of the ewes have died. They've got more than they can look after, and they'll sell them for a few shillings each."

"Oh, could we have one?" cried Victoria and Helen together.

"I should think so," I said. "You'd have to find out about feeding it, Geoffrey."

"We could use a baby's bottle at first," Geoffrey said. "They can have cow's milk, undiluted—I'll ask how much, and how often. We should have to get a bigger bottle and teat later on, and then it would eat grass. And when it grows up we could have it sheared and sell the wool."

"We shouldn't have to mow the lawn!" said Steven.

"We can get Snowy now," said Victoria happily.

Steven said hopefully, "Our landlord has got some puppies for sale too. They're black-and-white ones, only six weeks old. I *would* love to have a dog."

"I expect we could manage it," I sighed. "If you could train it not to worry the cats, or chase sheep."

"Chickens, and a cow, and Snowy—and a puppy and a lamb," said Helen, "and the cats and the rabbits—we shall have nearly a farm!"

"What shall we call it?" Steven asked.

"We shall have to think of a name," I said.

"What about The Farm on the Hill?" said Geoffrey.

"Or The Cottage in a Cornfield," suggested Steven.

"Green Pastures," contributed Victoria.

"Buttercup Farm," said Helen.

Christopher and Nicholas sat side by side on the hearthrug, looking intently at a picture of a tractor and plough. Carol, in her playpen, blew kisses to attract our attention, and held up her face to be kissed back.

"What do *you* think?" Geoffrey asked me.

"I know what I'd like to call it," I said, looking at my family gathered round me. "Harvest Home.